Will Allie ever feel comfortable in her new home?

"Everyone is trying so hard to make me feel okay," she told the animals, crouching down to rub Riley's head. Jinx hung his head over the stall door, chuffing warm air on the back of her neck. Even though the Thoroughbred had a nasty disposition, for some reason he had taken a liking to Allie and was perfectly mannered for her.

Allie straightened and stroked Jinx's glossy neck. "Everything here is so perfect," she told the colt. "Everything except that Mom and Dad aren't here." She slumped against the side of the stall, and Jinx rested his chin on her shoulder. A fresh layer of grayness seemed to enfold her, forming a sort of haze between the rest of the world and her. "It isn't that I'm not grateful," she told Jinx. "Everyone wants me feel at home, but I don't, and I don't know what to do about it."

Collect all the books in the Thoroughbred series

Collect all the books in the Ashleigh series

THOROUGHBRED Super Editions

ASHLEIGH'S Thoroughbred Collection

*coming soon

THOROUGHBRED

ALLIE'S LEGACY

CREATED BY

JOANNA CAMPBELL

WRITTEN BY

MARY NEWHALL

HarperEntertainment
An Imprint of HarperCollinsPublishers

♯ HarperEntertainment
An Imprint of HarperCollins*Publishers*
10 East 53rd Street, New York, NY 10022-5299

This is a work of fiction. The characters, incidents, and dialogue are products of the author's imagination and are not to be construed as real. Any resemblance to actual events or persons, living or dead, is entirely coincidental.

▦ Produced by 17th Street Productions, an Alloy Online, Inc., company

HarperCollins books are available at special quantity discounts for bulk purchases for sales promotions, premiums, or fund-raising. For information please call or write: Special Markets Department, HarperCollins Publishers Inc., 10 East 53rd Street, New York, NY 10022-5299. Telephone: (212) 207-7528. Fax: (212) 207-7222.

ISBN 0-06-075834-1

HarperCollins®, ♯®, and HarperEntertainment™ are trademarks of HarperCollins Publishers Inc.

First printing: March 2005

Printed in the United States of America

Visit HarperEntertainment on the World Wide Web at
www.harpercollins.com

❖ 10 9 8 7 6 5 4 3 2 1

For Lesley Ward—you rock!

ALLIE'S LEGACY

A GUST OF COLD JANUARY WIND WHIPPED ACROSS THE school parking lot, and Allie Avery wrapped her coat around her, hugging her schoolbooks to her chest. The weather in Kentucky was nothing like what she had known in Southern California. But then, nothing in Kentucky felt familiar, even though she'd been there for several months.

All around Allie, other students from Henry Clay High School were crowding up to the buses, talking and laughing. Allie felt like a rock in a stream, stuck in place while everything moved around her. But she couldn't stand there forever. If she missed the bus, she'd have to call her foster mother, Cindy McLean, to come and get her. But Cindy was busy at Tall Oaks, the Thoroughbred farm outside of Lexington she managed. Bothering Cindy for no reason wouldn't be very nice, considering all the things Cindy did for her, and the last thing Allie wanted to be was a burden. Even though losing her parents had been the most horrible thing in the world, if she had to live somewhere other than her own home, Tall Oaks was a good place to be.

Allie took a step toward the bus and was caught in the momentum of the students pushing toward the buses and the parking lot beyond. A sense of panic threatened to overwhelm her as she was pushed forward, and for a moment she fought to stand still.

Get a grip, Avery, she told herself sharply as the other students jostled her. *They just want to get on the bus and go home, and you're in the way.*

She climbed onto the bus, stopping near the driver while she looked for an empty seat. But she had waited too long. The whole length of the bus, there was at least one person in each seat.

"Hey, get going," a voice behind her said at the same time as someone nudged her, forcing Allie to step forward. She couldn't just stand there blocking the aisle, but where was she going to sit? If she picked a random seat, someone might be upset because they were saving it for a friend. Or worse, she might end up sitting next to some bully. She'd known some at her school in California, the kids who seemed to have radar for people with weaknesses. So far she hadn't come across anyone at Henry Clay who acted that way. But Allie knew that she was as full of self-doubt as Swiss cheese was full of holes, and that made her a good target.

She hadn't always been that way, but being orphaned at the age of fourteen had shaken her world. According to the counselor that California Children's Services had sent her to, it would take a long time before she felt sure of herself again. But even though it had been nearly eight months since her father's fatal accident, Allie still felt as though the world might turn upside down again at any moment. She reminded herself that at least she felt almost normal when she was around horses, and at Tall Oaks she was around them every day.

She took a deep breath, trying to force a feeling of confidence. She didn't have to be intimidated. Allie glanced to her side and saw a girl sitting by the window, waving at someone outside. Without a word,

Allie slipped into the empty half of the seat. *There,* she told herself. *You aren't a total wimp. The counselor would say that was definite progress.*

The other girl snapped her head away from the window and stared at Allie with a surprised look.

Allie felt her moment of confidence fade rapidly under the girl's piercing gaze. "Sorry," she said quickly. "I hope no one else was sitting here." She recognized the girl, another freshman, from her science class, although she couldn't remember her name at the moment.

"Why are you sorry?" The girl leaned her head back against the seat and rolled her eyes. "It isn't like I own the seat or anything. You can sit wherever you want, and no one can tell you any different. The taxpayers own the bus, and thanks to them, we get to ride it."

Allie wasn't sure how to respond to the comment. "Oh," she said lamely.

"My dad's a legislator," the girl continued. "That's about all we talk about at dinner. How to spend tax money wisely, who gets the most benefit from services, that kind of stuff." She tilted her head in Allie's direction. "You're new at Henry Clay, aren't you?"

Allie nodded. "I moved here from California last summer," she said. When she had first arrived at Tall Oaks,

Cindy had homeschooled her, giving her time to get used to all the changes that had occurred. After Thanksgiving she had started at Henry Clay, but just a few weeks later the school had closed for winter break. Then she had missed a few days for a trip to Florida for the Spectacular Bid Stakes. Her friend, jockey Melanie Graham, had invited her to come to help handle Melanie's three-year-old colt, Hi Jinx. The race had been exciting, especially since Melanie and Jinx had won.

Now Melanie was training Jinx for another Kentucky Derby prep race, and Allie was helping her work with the feisty chestnut colt. The thought of Jinx brightened Allie's dark mood. She could hardly wait until the next morning, when she would help Melanie exercise him again.

"Helloooo?" The girl's voice broke into Allie's thoughts. "Didn't you hear me?"

"I'm sorry, I was thinking about something else," Allie said, turning to face the other girl. *Is her name Laura or Linda? Maybe it's Libby.* Allie struggled to remember, but nothing sounded right.

"I asked why you moved here," Laura-Linda-Libby repeated. "Did your parents change their jobs?"

Allie sucked in a deep breath. She didn't want to explain how her mother had died of leukemia two years before and how her father had died in an accident on the racetrack the past summer. Allie didn't want sympathy, and she didn't want to talk about her parents. Every time she thought of Jilly Gordon, her mom, or Craig Avery, her dad, she felt so much aching inside that she couldn't stand it.

"I went to California on vacation last year," the other girl continued, relieving Allie of the need to answer the question. "San Diego was awesome. We went to the marine park, went shopping in Mexico, and went for a cruise on a huge yacht. If I got a chance to live there, I'd never come back to Kentucky."

Allie was starting to regret her choice of seats. The bus engine roared to life, and the driver pulled out of the parking lot, grinding the gears as he gained speed. Allie looked past the other girl at the scenery they were passing. There wasn't much to look at, just rows of houses as they passed out of the residential district. Soon they would be driving by horse farms, but Allie knew that with the cold, wet weather, most of the Thoroughbreds would be tucked away in the barns.

"My name's Lila," the other girl said suddenly. "I didn't catch your name."

"Allison," Allie replied politely. "Everyone calls me Allie."

Lila nodded. "You're in my science class. Doesn't Mr. Drummond make you nuts?"

Allie inhaled. She thought the science teacher was interesting. She liked the way he described the elements and how they fit in the periodic table, and she had caught herself laughing at some of his demonstrations. She wasn't sure if he made things go wrong on purpose or if he really was a bit of a mad scientist, but it kept her attention. She glanced at Lila, who was looking at her expectantly, and shrugged.

"It's a required class," she finally said. "Even if we don't like the teacher, we still have to take it."

Lila nodded. "I know," she said with a loud sigh. "But that doesn't mean I have to be excited about learning how to make sugar into a lump of charcoal." She frowned at Allie. "You said you've been here since last fall, but you've never ridden this bus before."

Allie nodded. "I'm going to a horse farm that belongs to some friends," she said.

"Which farm?" Lila asked. "I know most of them."

"Whisperwood," Allie told her. The farm, owned by Cindy's sister, Samantha, and her husband, Tor Nelson, focused on eventing and show jumping. Allie had spent several years taking jumping lessons in California, and she enjoyed working with the younger students at Tor and Samantha's farm. "My friend Christina Reese is teaching jumping lessons this afternoon, and I'm going to help her," she explained to Lila. She wouldn't be riding the bus that day, either, but Christina, who normally picked Allie up after school when they were going to give lessons, was at a doctor's appointment that afternoon.

"Ha!" Lila said, tossing her head. "Chris Reese is a jockey, not a riding teacher. She won the Belmont last summer. I saw it on TV." She narrowed her eyes. "So you moved out here from California to give riding lessons with a famous jockey? Yeah, right." She shook her head, then turned away from Allie to gaze out the window.

Allie stared down at her hands, feeling heat rise in her face. She wanted to tell Lila off, but the more she thought about it, the less she felt like explaining anything to the other girl.

She looked out the window, recognizing the area the bus was passing through. She picked up her backpack, preparing to get off the bus at the entrance to

Whisperwood. When the bus stopped and Allie rose, Lila darted her a look of surprise. "You really are getting off here?"

Allie nodded silently, then walked down the aisle, her chin lifted high. The wind caught her shoulder-length brown hair as she climbed from the bus, and she clutched her bag to her chest, eager to see Sterling Dream and Irish Battleship, two of her favorite mares.

A car pulled up behind the bus, its horn honking, and relief poured through Allie when she recognized the driver. Christina Reese stopped the car at the farm entrance and rolled down her window. "Hey, Allie!" Christina called with a grin. "How's this for perfect timing?"

Allie hurried toward the passenger side, but she glanced up as the bus roared away to see Lila staring out the window, a stunned look on her face. Allie hopped into the car and exhaled heavily, setting her pack on the seat beside her.

"Long day at school?" Christina asked, starting up the drive.

"Oh, no," Allie said quickly, pasting a bright smile on her face. She wasn't going to breathe a word of complaint about school or about how she felt like a total outsider. If she said anything, the social services people might decide she needed to live somewhere else. "School was fine. I'm just looking forward to some horse time."

Christina darted a sharp look in her direction, then nodded. "Me too," she said. "The doctor said it looks like I should be able to start riding again within a month. I'm so excited I can hardly stand it."

Christina had broken her ankle in an accident on the track several months before. Recovering from surgery had kept her firmly on the ground ever since Allie had met her, and Allie was looking forward to going for a ride with the older girl. Christina, who was Melanie's cousin, was one of the nicest people Allie had ever met. Even though Christina and Melanie had completely different personalities, both of them went out of their way to make Allie feel at home in Lexington.

As they pulled up to Whisperwood's big indoor arena, a red-haired woman came out the sliding door and waved at them. "Hi, Samantha," Allie said as she climbed from the car. She glanced at Samantha Nelson's round stomach, then gave the young farm owner a warning look. "You haven't been doing anything you shouldn't, have you?" Samantha was expecting twins within the next two months, and she had been told by the doctor to take it easy. Her husband, Tor, had given his own orders that everyone around Samantha was to keep a close eye on her in case she decided to do her regular chores.

"I've been lazy all day," Samantha announced, smiling at Allie. She rested her hands on her stomach. "The twins and I moved two tons of hay, cleaned eleven stalls, raked the arena, and groomed six horses. Then we had breakfast and took a nap."

Allie glanced at Christina, not sure if Samantha was teasing or if she really had done all those things.

"I'd believe you, Sammy," Christina said, hobbling on her cane as she came around the car. "But since Parker, Tor, Allie, Kevin, and Melanie got the hay barn in order last weekend, there wasn't so much as a wisp of hay for you to move." Christina's boyfriend, Parker Townsend, a world-class eventing competitor, taught advanced lessons at Whisperwood. Kevin McLean, Samantha and Cindy's younger brother, was working with his father training racehorses, and he was also helping Melanie with Jinx.

"And I know Kaitlin cleaned all the stalls yester-

11

day," Christina added. Kaitlin Boyce, a senior at Henry Clay, worked at Whisperwood to pay for her eventing lessons on Sterling Dream.

"But it sounded so productive," Samantha said with a grin. "I'm going to go stir-crazy waiting for these babies to show up."

"I know how you feel," Christina said, pointing the end of her cane at her foot in its padded shoe. "A couple of months doesn't sound like much time, but it sure drags."

"What do we need to do first?" Allie asked, standing in the open doorway and gazing at the open arena.

"The first lesson group should be here any minute," Samantha said, glancing at her watch. "Are you going to have the beginners do cavaletti work, Chris?"

"That's a good place to start," Christina said.

"I'll go lay out the poles," Allie announced, hurrying inside. She quickly set out the white-painted cavaletti poles, spacing them carefully so that the youngest students could trot their ponies over the low obstacles.

As she worked, some of the afternoon students began to arrive. Kaitlin walked in with several of the younger ones and immediately began helping them groom and tack their horses. Christina had followed

Samantha into her office, and Allie could hear laughter as the two women visited. The sound made her feel a little lonely. Christina and Samantha were so lucky to have so many people they were close to.

After her mother had died, Allie's father had assured her that all the people they knew at the track in California were just like family, so she would never really be alone. But when her father had died, none of those people was able to give her a home. Cindy had worked hard to get her to Kentucky and give her a place to live, but Allie knew that could end at any time, as the courts were trying to find any distant relatives who might be able to take her in.

Not knowing what was going to happen made it hard for Allie to feel settled at Tall Oaks. She knew it was wrong, but she found herself hoping that she had no family, which would make it easier for her to stay at the farm. She was determined to make herself indispensable so that everyone would want her to stay.

She quickly finished preparing the arena, then hurried over to where one of the kids was struggling to get her horse, a tall black gelding, to lower his head so that she could put his bridle on.

"Let me give you a hand, Gina," Allie said with a

friendly smile. "I know a little trick to get Tobin to drop his head for you and take the bit."

"Really?" The ten-year-old handed the bridle to Allie, who showed her how to get the horse to lower his head by holding her hand low so that he would reach his nose down to sniff at it. Then she slipped the headstall into place and handed the reins back to Gina.

"That was smart," Gina said admiringly. "Can you teach me some other things, like how to get him to pick up his feet easier so I can clean them?"

"Sure thing," Allie said, giving the girl a confident nod. "But right now you need to check your girth and mount up for your lesson."

The hour of helping the group of students sped by. After the last of the riders had left, Kaitlin brought Sterling Dream into the arena. Allie watched the older girl ride the big gray mare, wondering what it would be like to have a horse of her own again. But that wasn't going to happen, she reminded herself. She didn't have a permanent home herself, so she could hardly expect to have her own horse to work with. She would be happy with riding Samantha's jumpers and Cindy's racehorses.

"Do you want to saddle up Irish Battleship?"

Samantha asked, waddling up to where Allie was standing. "She could use a little work."

Allie glanced at the pretty redhead. "I'd like to, but I think Chris is ready to leave," she said when she saw Christina limping out of the office. She didn't have any other way to get back to Tall Oaks, and she didn't want to annoy Christina by making her wait. Besides, Cindy might have work for her to do at the other farm, and she did have a pile of homework. If her grades slipped at all, it might be reason enough for the courts to send her to another foster home.

"Are you ready to go?" Christina asked, limping over to Allie. "My foot is throbbing. I need to go prop it up for a while."

Allie nodded agreeably. "Sure thing," she said, turning to Samantha. "See you later," she said, then headed out of the arena as Kaitlin took Sterling over a small jump. Allie quickly looked away, stifling the jealous feeling that squeezed at her chest.

She gazed out the window on the ride home, trying to sort out her feelings. She loved Tall Oaks, but she felt guilty about enjoying the farm so much. If her parents were still alive, she wouldn't be there, so it seemed wrong to want to stay at the farm so badly.

"Is everything okay?" Christina asked as they sped along the two-lane road that led to Tall Oaks. "You seem a little down."

"I'm fine," Allie said quickly. "Just thinking about my schoolwork."

"Oh," Christina said in reply. After a moment of silence she glanced over at Allie. "If there's anything I can help you with . . ." She let her voice trail off. "I mean, like with tests or anything. I got pretty good grades in high school." Christina was attending college to become a veterinarian and working at a local clinic, so Allie was sure that if she needed help with math or science, Christina could help her out.

"Thanks for offering," Allie said, staring out the window. She wished her parents had never left Kentucky. If they had stayed there, maybe Jilly wouldn't have gotten sick, Craig wouldn't have been in the wreck that took his life, and she would have grown up around these people who were trying to be a replacement family for her. Instead she felt like a stranger to whom everyone was trying to be extra nice, and she just wanted to feel normal. But normal seemed an impossibly long way from where she was at the moment.

2

"HERE WE ARE," CHRISTINA ANNOUNCED AS SHE PULLED UP in front of Cindy's cottage. In the deepening twilight of the winter evening, the light that shone through the big front window made the little house look homey and inviting.

"Thanks for the ride," Allie said, gathering up her books. She paused before climbing out of the car. "Do you want to come in?" she asked. "I'm sure Cindy would like to see you."

"Not tonight," Christina said. "Tell Cindy hi, and I'll come by to visit when I'm not hurting so much."

"Feel better," Allie said as she got out. "Are you

sure you'll be up to teaching again tomorrow afternoon?"

"Definitely," Christina said. "I just need to elevate my foot. Too much walking around today took its toll."

"Well," Allie said before she closed the car door, "if there's anything I can do to help, will you tell me?"

"I'll be sure to let you know," Christina said, smiling warmly at her. "Thanks, Allie. You are a great kid. I'll pick you up after school tomorrow, okay?"

Allie flashed a smile, then shut the door and hurried up the walk to the house, which everyone referred to as Cindy's cottage. Then she looked up the hill at the huge colonial mansion where Ben al-Rihani, the owner of Tall Oaks, lived. Compared to the main house, the caretaker's cottage wasn't very big. But with its brick siding and slate roof, the cottage was the nicest house Allie had ever lived in. Her parents' priority had been working with horses, and they had never put a lot of time into fixing up their house in California.

Thinking of her parents dampened Allie's mood, but she tried to shove the bleak feeling away, reminding herself that Craig and Jilly would want her happy even without them. She swung the door open and went inside, stopping to glance around. Cindy had tried to tidy the living room, dusting some surfaces but missing others. On the coffee table in front of the soft, comfortable sofa lay a halter and lead rope. Apparently Cindy had forgotten she had them in her hands when she left the barn for the house. Allie picked up the pieces and set them by the door. She'd put them away later. She knew Cindy had enough on her mind, what with managing the farm and trying to be a foster parent, without having to deal with a little thing like putting some tack away.

Allie went to her room and set her books on the desk beside the computer, then looked around. Her bedroom was perfectly tidy, just as she had left it that morning. The bed was made, her laundry was in the hamper near the closet, and the book she had been reading was sitting on the nightstand next to a picture of her parents. She sighed.

In California, her room had usually been pretty messy. Her mother had kept after Allie to keep it neat, and now Allie wished she'd done better. She remembered her mother standing in the doorway, her hands on her hips. "I've seen you sweep cobwebs out of a stall, but you can't pick up your dirty socks?" Jilly had asked, shaking her head. "You're a horse person all the way, Miss Allison."

When her mother had gotten sick, Allie had helped her father with the housework. She had convinced herself that if she did everything perfectly, her mother would get better. But even though she had kept the house immaculate, it hadn't helped. As they watched helplessly the leukemia had slowly pulled Jilly away from them, and Allie and her father had quit caring about how clean the house was. They had spent every precious minute with her mother, doing everything they could think of to win the losing race against the terrible disease.

The memory brought a lump to Allie's throat, and she hurried from the room, not letting herself give in to the urge to cry. As she passed through the living room on the way to the kitchen, she stopped to pick a throw pillow off the floor, plumping it before she set it back on the couch. She looked around the haphazardly cleaned room and then turned her eyes skyward. *Cindy isn't much of a housekeeper, Mom, but you should see how clean her barn is.* Then she went through the little dining room and into the kitchen, where Cindy was standing in the middle of the room, a wooden spoon in one hand and a cookbook in the other.

"You're home!" Cindy exclaimed. "I didn't expect you quite so soon." She set down the cookbook. "I was trying to get dinner ready, but things aren't going too smoothly."

Allie looked around the room. Every counter was covered with cooking utensils and empty packages and bags. The stove was spattered with tomato sauce, and the floor was littered with broken spaghetti noodles.

Since Allie had been living with Cindy, their usual meals were frozen entrees, take-out food, or leftovers from dinner at Ben's, where the cook prepared multi-course gourmet meals. Allie looked at Cindy with a questioning expression.

Cindy shrugged and grinned. "I wanted to fix us a nice dinner," she said. "But I think I'm allergic to kitchen work."

They both jumped as a loud sizzling sound came from the stove top. "Oh, no!" Cindy yelped, darting to the stove, where a pot of spaghetti was boiling over. "Ugh." She groaned, stirring the pasta with the wooden spoon. "Most of them stuck to the bottom of

21

the pot. I wonder if Riley would eat burned spaghetti," Cindy mused, carrying the ruined pot of noodles to the sink. Riley, the dog who was Jinx's stable companion, had befriended Allie and seemed to spend as much time with her as he did with the colt.

"I doubt it," Allie said, eyeing the disaster area. "I could help," she offered. "I used to cook for my dad all the time." The memory of her old life, forever gone, made her throat constrict again, and she swallowed hard. Every time she thought she had her feelings under control, some random memory would bring the sadness back.

After her mom had died, her father had struggled to make things feel normal. But losing Jilly had left a gaping hole in their lives. Gradually Allie and her father had figured out ways to work together, but just as they were developing a routine that felt comfortable, the horrible accident on the track had taken him. Allie felt as if her life had been struck by an earthquake that made California's worst disasters seem mild.

She glanced up to see Cindy watching her, and she forced another of her bright smiles. "If you wash the pan and boil more water, I'll stir the sauce and toast some garlic bread," she said. "We can have a green salad, too. That would be simple to fix."

Cindy's worried expression faded, and she nodded. "I'll let you be the boss," she replied.

"Maybe I can teach you how to cook," Allie said.

Cindy looked around the kitchen and raised her eyebrows. "I'm afraid I'm beyond hope," she said. "But you can try."

When they finally sat down to eat, Cindy smiled across the kitchen table at Allie. "Thanks for bailing me out," she said. "With your help, I'll figure out how to be a good mom."

"You're doing great," Allie reassured her. She took a bite of salad and sat back. Her bleak mood had lifted while she was helping Cindy in the kitchen. Working together to fix dinner had been fun.

After dinner Allie started to clear the table, but Cindy raised a hand to stop her. "I'll do the dishes," Cindy said. "After all, you did most of the cooking."

"Are you sure?" Allie asked. "I don't mind." She didn't want Cindy to think she was avoiding any responsibilities. From the kitchen window she could see the security lights shining in front of the barn. She wouldn't mind going out to the barn before she did her schoolwork, but she hesitated, eyeing Cindy doubtfully.

"Really," Cindy said, taking a barn coat from a hook by the kitchen door and draping it over Allie's shoulders. "Go tuck Jinx in before you do your homework."

Allie thrust her arms into the sleeves and stuffed her hands in the pockets as she walked down to the barn. Overhead, the sky was a deep, cloudless black, studded with twinkling stars. Allie gazed at the constellations for a minute before going inside the barn. Her father had taught her the names of the stars, and she comforted herself with the thought that her parents were up there somewhere, watching over her.

The wide aisle of the barn was swept clean, and the low lights along the walls pushed the shadows back. Allie inhaled, taking in the sweet smell of horses, hay, and clean leather. She strolled down the aisle of the main barn, pausing to pet Rush Street, the bay stallion she exercised in the mornings, then walked to Jinx's stall, where she found Riley lying in front of the door. The little brown-and-white dog sat up when he saw her, his tail thumping the floor in excitement. Jinx lifted his gleaming chestnut head and bobbed his nose at her, inhaling her scent deeply.

"Everyone is trying so hard to make me feel okay," she told the animals, crouching down to rub Riley's head. Jinx hung his head over the stall door, chuffing warm air on the back of her neck. Even though the Thoroughbred had a nasty disposition, for some reason he had taken a liking to Allie and was perfectly mannered for her.

Allie straightened and stroked Jinx's glossy neck. "Everything here is so perfect," she told the colt. "Everything except that Mom and Dad aren't here." She slumped against the side of the stall, and Jinx rested his chin on her shoulder. A fresh layer of grayness seemed to enfold her, forming a sort of haze between the rest of the world and her. "It isn't that I'm not grateful," she told Jinx. "Everyone wants me feel at home, but I don't, and I don't know what to do about it."

She heard footsteps in the aisle and stood up, looking down the long row of stalls to see who was coming. Beckie, the young groom who had moved to Kentucky from Australia, was striding past the stalls, pausing occasionally to pet one of the horses. When she saw Allie, she smiled, waving cheerfully. "Hi, Allie," she said, stopping at Jinx's stall. The colt pinned back his ears at her, and Beckie shook her head in disgust. "I'm sure glad you two get along," she told Allie. "No matter what I do for that brat, he's just waiting for the chance to trample me into the ground." She rolled her eyes. "You have a special way with him, y'know."

Allie glanced at Jinx, then ran her hand along his neck. "I guess we understand each other," she said. "He's just defensive and doesn't trust people to get too close."

"I think it's more than that," Beckie said. "There's something about you that the animals connect with. You've got a gift."

Allie smiled, feeling the bleakness fade a little. "Thanks, Beckie," she said. "I'd better get back to the house. I have a ton of homework to do."

"I'm heading home, too," Beckie said. "There's a special on TV about the wild horses of Africa I want to see."

As Beckie turned to leave, Allie took a deep breath. "Do you miss your family?" she asked quickly, before she lost her courage to ask the personal question. "Don't you get homesick?"

Beckie stopped and turned slowly, then tilted her

head thoughtfully. "I do at times," she said. "But I feel like this is my home now. It was scary to leave Dardanup, the town I grew up in, but my mum and dad did everything they could to help me be independent. They were happy I had a chance to come to the United States and work here." She paused. "You must hurt terribly, with both your folks gone."

Allie shrugged. "Everyone tells me it's going to take some time to get over it," she said. "But most days I feel like I'll never get there."

Beckie frowned. "My gram, my mom's mom, lived with us for years, and we used to sit outside every evening to watch the sunset. She's the one who taught me what I know about horses. When she passed away, I thought I'd never again enjoy anything that reminded me of her." She gazed at Allie for a minute. "But after a while I started looking forward to seeing the sunsets and grooming the horses again."

"Even though it made you think of her?" Allie asked.

Beckie shook her head. "*Because* it made me think of her," she replied. "Now you'd better get off to the cottage so I don't get in trouble for keeping you from your schoolwork. I'll see you tomorrow."

After Beckie left the barn, Allie gave Jinx one last pat, bent down to ruffle Riley's floppy ears, then walked back to the cottage. She stopped several yards from the house, looking at the warm yellow glow in the windows, and for a moment Allie imagined walking inside to find both her parents sitting in the living room. Her dad would be doing some leatherworking, his favorite hobby, and her mother would be knitting. Not that Jilly had ever finished a knitting project, Allie recalled, smiling at the memory of her father's comments. "If you just kept working on one scarf," he would say, "you could make one that would circle the globe."

Jilly would wrinkle her nose. "I know what I'm doing," she would say. "Someday I'm going to sew all these strips together and make Allie a nice blanket."

At that thought, Allie's mood shifted downward again. Someday had never come, and she didn't know what had happened to her mother's bag of knitting when she had been shipped off to Kentucky. Other people had taken care of all the things left at her parents' house.

She shook her head, trying to rid herself of the sadness she was feeling, and strode up to the house. When she opened the front door, she could hear voices in the kitchen. From where she stood, she could see Ben and Cindy sitting at the kitchen table, talking.

Not wanting to interrupt them, Allie slipped quietly into her bedroom and laid out her homework. She felt a lot of pressure to get perfect grades so that no one could use her school performance as a reason to send her someplace else. Maybe she didn't feel really settled at Tall Oaks, but she knew she'd never have a better home than this.

She started with math, racing through the easier algebra problems, finally setting her finished paper aside with a relieved sigh. Algebra wasn't her favorite class, but so far she had been able to keep up and not ask for help. She rose, stretching her cramped shoulder muscles, and pressed her hand to her stomach. A glass of milk and one of the pecan cookies Ben's chef had sent down the day before would be a good reward for the work she'd done.

Allie left her room and walked past Cindy's desk, tucked in a corner of the living room, stopping when she noticed an envelope with social services' return address on the corner. She paused, then glanced toward the kitchen. She could hear the soft murmur of

Ben and Cindy's voices, then laughter as Ben said something that amused Cindy. She looked at the envelope again. Of course it would be about her, even though it was addressed to Cindy, so it would probably be all right for her to look at it. She slipped the letter out and began reading.

Dear Ms. McLean:

As we have discussed over the past several weeks, our office has continued to search for any relatives of Allison Avery's. We may have found a cousin of Jilly Gordon's, Gail Hickam, in New York, and will keep in touch with you regarding our progress in this matter. It is our priority to place Allison with biological family if at all possible. In the meantime, Allison will continue to stay with you as long as she is thriving under your care.

Allie felt her stomach lurch, and she quickly refolded the letter, stuffing it away. Her hands were shaking, and her heart seemed to stutter. She hadn't even known her mom had a cousin. If her mom had never mentioned it, they must not have been very close.

Allie had known all about the people in Kentucky. She had heard stories of Whitebrook, the farm owned by Christina's parents, jockey Ashleigh Griffin and her husband, Mike Reese. She knew all about Samantha and Cindy, who had grown up at Whitebrook, so she'd felt she knew them at least a little before she came here. What would Gail Hickam be like? Was she a horse person? Did she live in a little apartment in the middle of the city? Was she nice, or some grumpy old woman who hated kids?

The voices in the kitchen grew louder as Ben and Cindy left the kitchen table. Allie stepped away from the desk, planting a smile on her face as Ben came into the living room, his jacket over his arm.

"Good evening, Allie," he said.

"Hi," Allie said, unable to help feeling a little shy around the farm owner. She never knew whether to call him Ben or Mr. al-Rihani, and she used every bit of good manners she knew when she was around him. Tall, dark, and handsome, Ben had grown up in the United Arab Emirates, where his father, a wealthy sheik, had owned a Thoroughbred stable. Ben was always polite and friendly to her, never acting like a rich snob, and Allie appreciated his courtesy. But it was intimidating to be around someone with Ben's wealth and power.

"You look a little distraught," Ben said, eyeing her curiously as Cindy came into the room.

Allie shook her head quickly. "I'm just tired," she said firmly, trying to make her smile as pleasant as she could. "I had a lot of homework to do. I was just coming out to say good night."

Ben and Cindy exchanged a look that reminded Allie of her parents when they thought she wasn't telling them the whole story, but neither Ben nor Cindy questioned her.

"There are still a few cookies left," Cindy told her. "Do you want a bedtime snack?"

But the social services letter had killed Allie's appetite, and she shook her head. "I'm not hungry, thanks," she said. "I'll see you in the morning."

She returned to her room, donning her pajamas before she brushed her teeth and washed her face, following the familiar bedtime ritual her mother and father had established when she was little. When she climbed into bed, she looked at the photo of her parents on the nightstand and felt hot tears welling up behind her eyes.

"Why did you have to leave me?" she whispered, reaching out to touch the glass that covered the picture. The cold hardness reminded her that she would never be able to touch them again, and she buried her face in her pillow, determined to muffle her sobs. She went to sleep with salty tears burning her cheeks, wishing she could wake up to find that losing her parents had been nothing worse than a terrible nightmare.

3

ALLIE'S EYES WERE STILL SWOLLEN FROM CRYING WHEN HER alarm went off the next morning. She stumbled to the bathroom, and when she looked in the mirror, her skin was blotchy and her eyes red and puffy.

"That doesn't look good," she muttered, holding a wet washcloth to her face. "If Cindy thinks I'm crying myself to sleep, she'll assume I'm not happy here and tell the social worker."

She rinsed the cloth and pressed it to her eyes again, and after several minutes her face looked better. She dressed quickly, determined to be at the barn first thing. She had work to do before school, and she didn't want anyone to think she was lazy.

The house was still dark when she left her bedroom. She paused by the door to pick up the halter and lead that Cindy had brought to the house, then peeked in the kitchen. The automatic coffeemaker had already brewed a pot of coffee, and Allie eyed the carafe, half tempted to pour herself a cup to wake up. It smelled wonderful, but she'd had a sip or two of her dad's coffee on occasion, and it had tasted horrible—bitter and strong, nothing like the way it smelled. She grabbed a banana from the fruit bowl instead, then stuffed a large red apple in her jacket pocket and headed for the barn, peeling the banana as she walked. The security lights cast a glow over the front of the big stable with its ornamental stone siding and tall cupolas reaching toward the sky. Allie slid the barn door open so that she could slip inside.

She walked past Cindy's office, which was still dark, stopping in the tack room to hang the halter and lead rope on the rack. Before going to see Jinx and Rush Street, she headed down the wing of the barn where the fillies were kept. She paused at the first stall, where a small chestnut filly thrust her nose into the aisle and nickered low in her throat. "Hi there, sweetie," Allie said, stopping to pet the two-year-old

Thoroughbred's smooth neck. Ben and Cindy had purchased the filly at the Keeneland yearling auction the previous September.

Although Alpine Meadow was small by Thoroughbred standards, Cindy had been determined to own the filly. "I wanted her because she's out of Meadow Star," she had told Allie.

Allie was puzzled by Cindy's determination to own the filly. She knew very little about Meadow Star except that the mare had been the champion two-year-old, then Florida's champion three-year-old filly, but her four-year-old season had been unspectacular. Allie had thought Ben and Cindy wanted only top-notch racehorses. But Cindy's sole explanation for wanting the filly was because of her dam, which made Allie curious about the mare.

Allie liked Alpine Meadow, who was the sweetest horse she had ever met. The little chestnut had bright, intelligent eyes, and she "talked," emitting soft grunts and nickers, shoving her nose at Allie and demanding affection, which Allie gladly gave her.

Alpine squealed at her now, and Allie pulled the apple from her pocket, using her teeth to tear off a piece, which she handed to the filly.

Alpine Meadow gently lifted the chunk of apple and chewed it contentedly. "I have work to do," Allie told the filly. "But I'll come and visit later."

She stopped to pet the other auction filly Cindy had bought, a big-framed bay with a white snip on her nose, and then passed several empty stalls. She could imagine what the farm had been like in the past, thriving and successful, with beautiful Thoroughbreds in all the paddocks and employees hurrying about taking care of the horses. She sighed. Maybe, if she was lucky, she'd be around long enough to see it like that. But she knew Ben and Cindy's plan of restoring Tall Oaks to its former status as a top Thoroughbred racing farm was going to take several years, and she didn't know if she'd still be at the farm come summer.

The thought darkened her mood again, and she tried to clear her mind. She had a special horse to take care of, and she didn't need to let her mood affect Perfect Image.

She stopped at the big black filly's stall. Image was dozing, her head down and her ears relaxed. "Hey there, Image," Allie said in a soft voice.

Image blinked and raised her head, then gave a throaty nicker when she saw Allie. "I brought you a little goodie," Allie said, pulling the apple from her pocket again. "Sorry about the missing bite, but one of your stablemates asked for a little piece, and I couldn't say no."

She bit another chunk out of the apple and fed it to Image, who chomped it eagerly, then shoved her nose at Allie, looking for more.

"You have no manners!" Allie exclaimed, feeding Image another piece of apple. "I need to check your bandage and walk you out a bit, girl. You can have the rest of the apple when we're done."

Perfect Image had been bred at Tall Oaks, long before Ben bought the farm. Melanie's father, Will Graham, had partnered with one of the musicians he promoted, buying the filly for Melanie to train and race. Last year Melanie had ridden Perfect Image to a win in the Kentucky Derby, but at the end of the race the filly had collapsed with a broken leg. After months of therapy, she was slowly healing. Jazz Taylor, the rock star who had bought out the Grahams' interest in the filly, had recently sold her to Ben. When Image was ready, Cindy planned to breed her to Wonder's Champion, the Triple Crown–winning stallion she and Ben owned.

"You two will have an incredible baby," Allie told Image, clipping a lead onto her halter. She felt as though Melanie had given her a wonderful gift in letting her care for Image. Melanie adored the filly, and Allie knew she wouldn't let just anyone handle her. But for the time being, Melanie was dashing between Tall Oaks and Whitebrook, where she lived, doing double duty as an exercise rider until Christina could start riding again.

Allie gave a light tug on the lead, and Image came out of the stall easily. She let the girl cross-tie her, then stood quietly while Allie removed the supportive bandage from her foreleg. "You've gotten really used to this, haven't you?" Allie asked, replacing the bandage and checking to make sure it was snug but not too tight. Dr. Lanum, the vet who was caring for Image, had shown Allie how to wrap the leg properly. Allie liked Dr. Lanum, who talked to Allie as though she were an adult and perfectly capable of taking care of the valuable filly.

"Let's go for a stroll," she told Image, unclipping the ties so that she could walk the filly down the barn aisle. "As soon as the weather warms up again, we'll take some nice walks out past the paddocks." But once again the thought came to her mind that she might not be around to do that.

As soon as she was finished with Image, Allie fed the filly the rest of the apple and went in search of Elizabeth, the head groom, to see what needed to be done. Soon she was busy mixing feed, pushing a wheelbarrow filled with cans of different grains and vitamin supplements for the different horses. Beckie had already filled most of the hay nets, and Allie followed, pouring the grain into the horses' feed pans.

"Hey, are you going to ride with me this morning?" Melanie popped her head out of the tack room as Allie walked by with the wheelbarrow, the empty grain cans rattling. Allie stopped and looked at Melanie, her eyes wide with surprise.

"Of course I'm going to ride!" she said. "I haven't been on a horse since yesterday morning, and I miss it."

Melanie laughed. "Yeah," she agreed. "Once every twenty-four hours is hardly enough riding. I'll see you at the track."

Allie got Rush Street's bridle and the exercise saddle she used from the tack room and quickly readied the bay colt for his morning work. When she led him out to the practice track, Melanie was holding Jinx and talking to Kevin McLean. The red-haired trainer smiled broadly when he looked up and saw Allie.

"My favorite exercise rider," he greeted her. "Are you ready to work?"

"Yes, sir," Allie said firmly. "And when you get more horses at the Kevin McLean Training Stables, I'll ride them for you, too."

Kevin glanced at Jinx, then back at Allie. "So far we've just got Jinx," he said, shaking his head. "I guess I'll just have to keep helping my dad train over at Whitebrook for a while longer."

"At least until the Kentucky Derby," Allie said quickly. "Once Jinx wins the race, you'll be in big demand."

"I like Allie," Kevin said, turning to Melanie. "She's a good judge of quality horseflesh." He boosted Melanie onto Jinx's back, then turned to give Allie a leg up, and soon the girls had the horses on the track, walking them around the oval to warm them up.

Allie sat straight in the saddle, enjoying the feel of Rush Street's smooth strides. The colt, while not a champion racehorse, had a good personality and was easy to ride. Even though it was cold and dark, the track was well lit by vapor lights. Allie was warm in her hooded sweatshirt, riding gloves, and thick wool socks.

"I really appreciate your riding with me," Melanie said as they walked the horses along the outside rail. "Jinx does so much better when you're around."

"When Riley and I are around, you mean," Allie said.

"And Riley," Melanie agreed, glancing outside the oval, where the little dog was sitting beside Kevin, watching them closely. "It was like a miracle when you got to Florida and Jinx straightened right up. I never thought I was going to get him on the track for the Spectacular Bid." She smiled at Allie. "I really owe you."

"No, you don't," Allie replied quickly, shaking her head. "I'm just glad I was able to help. It was so cool being part of the team and seeing Jinx win the race."

"We'll be heading to Gulfstream again next month for the Fountain of Youth Stakes," Melanie said, keeping her attention on Jinx. But with Allie riding beside him, the colt was agreeable and attentive. "Kevin and I decided that would be a good prep race for him before the Derby. I hope you'll be able to go with us. I think you're Jinx's good-luck charm."

"Thanks," Allie said, trying not to feel over-whelmed by the confidence Melanie had in her ability to keep Jinx in line.

"I'll talk to Cindy about it," Melanie said. "Now let's pick up the pace a bit and give these boys a chance to stretch their legs."

The brisk gallop felt wonderful, but riding around the track made Allie think of her father again. She grimaced with frustration. It was so hard to love the horses as much as she did, yet know that racing was the reason she was an orphan. She couldn't get her thoughts off her father, and she ended the work with that dark cloud enfolding her again.

"I'll see you guys later," she told Melanie and Kevin when they brought the horses off the track to cool them down. "I'll get Rush Street taken care of, then I have to get ready for school."

"Are you all right?" Kevin asked, looking at her closely, a frown wrinkling his forehead.

"I'm fine," Allie said promptly, looking away from him to loosen Rush Street's girth. "I just have to get going."

She led the colt away, and as soon as he was cooled out, she returned him to his stall and fed him his morning rations, then trudged back up to the cottage. Cindy would be at the barn, so she didn't have to worry about her noticing if she was in a down mood.

The quiet of the cottage pressed around her, and Allie showered quickly, dressed in jeans and a sweater, and then sat down in the kitchen to eat a bowl of cereal before she walked down to catch the bus.

The sky was just starting to get light when the bus stopped at Tall Oaks' drive, and Allie hurried onto it, sitting in an empty seat near the front. She gazed out the window as they chugged along the country road, staring at the vast, white-fenced pastures and stately mansions and barns they passed. She barely noticed the stops the driver made, and the voices of the students getting on the bus sounded muffled and distant. She brooded about her home in Southern California and the life she had left behind.

"If you keep your nose pressed against the glass, it'll get flat on the end."

Allie jumped away from the window and snapped her head around to see a boy looking at her from across the aisle. He was about her age, with brown hair and a lanky build.

"You're Allie, right?" he asked.

She nodded silently, wondering who he was.

"I'm Jason Edwards," he told her. "I sit two seats behind you in history."

"I think I remember you," Allie said politely, embarrassed.

"You live at Tall Oaks, don't you?" Jason asked. "Is your dad that rich guy from the United Arab Emirates who bought the old farm last year?"

Allie hesitated. "No," she finally said. "My mom is the manager of the farm."

"Cool," Jason said, turning sideways and leaning forward, his long legs sticking into the aisle. "My dad works in the track office at Keeneland."

"Cindy bought two fillies at the auction last fall," Allie said, happy to have a safe subject to talk about.

"You call your mom by her first name?" Jason asked, giving her a puzzled look.

Allie felt herself sag. "No," she said slowly. "Cindy's my foster mom."

"Oh," Jason said, giving her a curious look. "Did you get in some kind of trouble that you got stuck in a foster home?"

Allie felt herself go cold. "No," she said. "I'm not in any trouble."

Jason shrugged. "I guess you won't be around here long if you're just in foster care, will you?"

Allie swallowed hard and straightened her back. Both her parents had been tough, competitive jockeys. They wouldn't have let a comment like that bother them. But Allie knew she wasn't as strong as either of her parents had been. She wished she had them to lean on now, when she needed them so much.

She tacked a prim smile on her face and raised her chin, looking down her nose at Jason. "Probably not," she said, trying to sound like she didn't care. "But you know, being a foster kid isn't so bad. You get to see how a lot of different families live."

"That would stink," Jason said.

"You just have to learn to live with it," Allie replied, tossing her hair back. Then she turned her back on Jason and fixed her gaze on the passing scenery, trying not to let her fears and weakness show through. She'd get through this, and no matter what happened, she'd be okay . . . wouldn't she?

4

ALLIE WALKED INTO HER SCIENCE CLASS WITH HER CHIN UP and her back straight and stiff, determined not to talk to anyone. After Lila had laughed at her the day before and Jason had made those comments on the bus that morning, she thought it was just as well not to try making friends at Henry Clay. She sat down and opened her textbook to the current chapter, staring down at the page while she waited for Mr. Drummond to start class.

"Hey, Allie."

She stiffened when she heard Lila's voice, and pretended to be so absorbed in her reading that she didn't hear the other girl. But from the corner of her eye she could see Lila standing beside her, and she looked up slowly, bracing herself for whatever Lila was going to say.

Lila offered her a nervous smile. "I wanted to apologize for yesterday," she said in a quiet voice. "I wasn't trying to make fun of you or anything."

Allie softened a bit. "That's okay," she said, then started to look down at her book again.

"No, it wasn't," Lila said insistently. "It's just that so many people make up stories to make themselves look better."

Allie glanced up at Lila, puzzled. "Why would they do that?" she asked.

Lila shrugged. "I told you, my dad is in politics. He always says to watch what people do, not what they say. I just didn't give you a chance, and I'm really sorry."

Allie sighed. Just when she thought she was going to be able to avoid liking anyone at Henry Clay, Lila caught her by surprise. She smiled at the other girl. "Really," she said. "It's okay."

Lila sat at the empty desk next to hers and leaned forward. "If you want to, you can have lunch with my friends and me," she said. "We sit at the corner table in the cafeteria."

Allie leaned back, startled by the offer. If she said no, she'd be insulting Lila, and she didn't want to offend anyone. On the other hand, she didn't want to get too friendly with a bunch of girls she might not ever see again if social services made her move. But she was getting tired of eating alone, and Lila was trying to be nice. She nodded to the other girl. "The corner table," she repeated. "I'll see you at lunch."

"Everyone in their own seats," Mr. Drummond said loudly from the front of the classroom.

Lila jumped up, pausing before she returned to her assigned seat. "I'll see you at lunch," she said, then walked away.

Allie spent her next two classes worrying about what might happen during lunch. Was Lila only pretending to be nice so that she and her friends would get a chance to make fun of the new girl? Allie didn't think so, but still, she was anxious, and by the time she went to her locker to get her food, she was so stressed that she could barely dial the combination to get the locker open. Finally the lock clicked free, and she shoved her books onto the shelf and grabbed her lunch bag.

She hurried to the cafeteria, scanning the large room until she spotted the corner table. Lila and four other girls were sitting together, and when Allie crossed the room, Lila smiled and waved at her. "I thought maybe you'd found something else to do," she said when Allie reached the table. "Have a seat." She waved at an empty spot.

As Allie settled on the bench, Lila introduced her to the crowd. "Abby, Brittany, Roxanne, and Kendra," she said, pointing at each one in turn.

"Hi, everyone," Allie said politely, trying to remember all the names. The other girls were already eating, so she opened her lunch bag and pulled out the sandwich Luis, Ben's chef, had prepared for her. When Cindy had handed Allie a bag lunch on her first day at Henry Clay, the younger girl had been overwhelmed by the gourmet meal Luis had prepared. "I can make a sandwich for myself," she'd told Cindy. "He doesn't have to do this."

"He wants to," Cindy had said. "Luis asked Ben if he could do something for you. If you told him you didn't want his lunches, you'd hurt his feelings."

Allie liked the chef, so she had accepted the fact that she was going to get sandwiches layered with specialty meats, cheeses, and vegetables on freshly baked rolls, accompanied by little containers of exotic salads and decoratively cut fresh fruits. Now, as she pulled the lid off her salad of watercress and marinated beets and opened the little tub of Luis's special dressing, Roxanne stared across the table, her mouth slack.

"Can I come and live at your house?" the plump blonde asked. "My mom gives me a carton of yogurt and tuna salad sandwiches. If that's what you get in your lunch, I'd love to be there for dinner."

Allie cringed, trying to think of how to explain about the fancy food. If she said a chef fixed her lunches, she'd sound like a snob. Instead she grinned across the table at Roxanne and told the story of Cindy's spaghetti disaster. The girls laughed.

"The only thing my mom can cook is meatloaf," Brittany said, nodding in understanding. "My dad does the cooking at our house."

Lila cocked her head. "Your mom does a mean grilled-cheese sandwich, too," she reminded Brittany. "My mom likes to cook, and since she and my dad entertain a lot, she has about a hundred cookbooks she's always looking through."

Allie began to relax, feeling a little more comfortable as the girls joked and teased each other. The lunch period passed quickly. When the girls got up to leave for their next class, Kendra paused, waiting for the others to go. "Your dad was Craig Avery," she said to Allie. "My dad trains for Millwood Farm. He knew your dad, and he was really sorry to hear about what happened. He said both your parents were great riders."

Allie avoided looking at Kendra, instead busying herself stuffing the empty food containers into her lunch bag. "Tell him thank you," she said, not sure if that was the correct response.

"Are you going to have lunch with us tomorrow?" Kendra asked. "You can if you want."

"Thanks," Allie said, glancing up at the other girl, afraid she was going to see pity in Kendra's expression. She didn't want anyone feeling sorry for her.

But Kendra just offered her a friendly smile and added with a wink, "Although you might think about packing more food. I thought Roxie was going to dive across the table to get that peach cobbler you had."

Allie laughed, feeling her tension fade. "Maybe I'll see you tomorrow at lunch," she said, then left the cafeteria to get her books for her afternoon classes. The rest of the day flew by. Allie kept thinking about the new friends she had made until school ended for the day, when she remembered her vow not to get too close to anyone at the high school. She walked out to the parking lot, where Christina was waiting for her.

"I had a great day at school," Christina announced when Allie climbed into the car. "How about you?"

Allie was quiet for a minute. "It was good," she finally said.

"You don't sound too sure about that," Christina commented. "Is there something bothering you?"

Allie thought about the letter from social services. "Can I tell you something, and you won't talk about it with Cindy?" she asked.

Christina took her hands off the steering wheel and turned to face Allie. "This sounds serious," she said.

Allie took a deep breath, then quickly told Christina about reading the letter and about her mother's cousin.

Christina looked thoughtful. "I would have done the same thing," she told Allie. "But if you're worried about what's going on, maybe you should ask Cindy about it."

Allie nodded. "You're right," she said. "But she'll be mad at me for reading her mail."

"Maybe," Christina said. "But I know Cindy, and I'm really sure she'll understand. She's told me stories about when she came to Whitebrook. Did you know that she ran away from a foster home, and Samantha found her sleeping in a stall with one of our foals?"

Allie shook her head, amazed. "Cindy did that?"

"Oh, yes," Christina said, nodding vigorously. "If you ask, I'm sure she'll tell you what she went through as a foster kid, and I know she doesn't want you to go through anything like what she did."

Allie felt better about approaching Cindy, and she gave Christina a relieved smile. "I'll talk to her," she promised.

"As soon as we're done at Whisperwood," Christina reminded her, putting the car into gear and pulling out of the parking lot. "We have work to do, kiddo."

Christina's boyfriend, Parker Townsend, was at Whisperwood when they arrived, He was riding one of his eventing horses, Wizard of Oz, in the arena. Allie watched in amazement as Parker, bareback astride the big horse, sailed over several jumps, making it look as though he and his horse were one.

"Wow," she murmured to Christina, who stood beside her against the arena wall.

"I know," Christina said admiringly. "He's the best rider I've ever seen. He's definitely going to be a member of the next Olympic team." Allie glanced at her as she gazed at Parker and Ozzie. Christina had a wistful look on her face. "If I'd stuck with eventing, we'd be competing together," she said.

"Do you miss it?" Allie asked. "I thought you loved being a jockey."

"I do," Christina said quickly. "I'm not sorry I picked racing, but sometimes I wonder what would have happened if I'd continued with eventing instead."

Allie thought about her own riding experiences. She had always loved racing, but after her father's fatal accident, she wasn't sure she would ever want to try being a jockey. Samantha had some incredible hunters at Whisperwood, and she could ride there as often as she wanted.

Parker brought Ozzie, as they called the horse, to a stop and slid from his tall back. He led the big jumper to where Allie and Christina were standing, bowed to them, then gestured at Ozzie. "Isn't he awesome?" he asked.

"You were awesome together," Christina replied,

patting Ozzie's muscled neck. "He sure isn't the same horse you brought home last year."

Allie knew that Ozzie had been burned out on eventing when Parker got him, but after a lot of hard work, Parker had figured out how to motivate the talented jumper. Now he was careful to keep Ozzie's training interesting and challenging, and his efforts were paying off.

Allie smiled at Christina's tall, dark-haired boyfriend. "You're really, really good," she said. "I wish I could ride that well."

Parker glanced at his watch. "The first class isn't going to start for another hour. Go get Irish Battleship out and I'll give you a quick lesson."

"Really?" Allie felt a rush of excitement. "A private lesson with the greatest rider on the U.S. Equestrian Team?"

Parker laughed. "I wish I were," he said. "But I'll try to help you learn what I know."

Allie hurried off to tack up the big mare, eager to take her over the course Parker had set up. Soon she was riding Irish Battleship around the arena, warming up the mare. Samantha came into the arena and stood with Christina and Parker. Allie felt self-conscious with the three experienced riders watching her, and she put every bit of effort she could into riding well.

"Move with her," Parker called. "Balance, balance, balance."

Allie grimaced, trying to focus on her seat, back, legs, and hands while staying attentive to Irish Battleship, too. As they sailed over a four-foot fence she tried to concentrate on every detail of her jumping position. The brief, exhilarating moment of weightlessness made it worthwhile, and when they landed, she focused on the mare's strides, adjusting her weight and hand position to work with the talented eventing horse.

"Great one," Parker called. "Try it again, and this time relax a little."

Allie almost laughed. How was she supposed to relax and do everything perfectly? She did several more jumps, with Parker calling encouragement and offering her pointers, and when she finished riding, she was breathless, her face warm from the work. She heard the phone ring in Samantha's office, and the stable owner walked off as Allie rode her horse over to where Parker and Christina waited.

"I'm afraid you're going to make more competition

for me," Parker told her as she hopped from Irish Battleship's back.

"Never!" Allie exclaimed, shaking her head. "If you hadn't been coaching me through every jump, I never would have done that well." She patted the mare's sweaty neck. "I'd better get her cooled out before the students get here."

"I'll change the arena course for lessons," Parker said.

"I'll tell you how," Christina said jokingly, waving her cane. "I love hard work. I could stand here and watch people do it all day long."

Parker rolled his eyes. "I know it kills you to stand still while I do the work. I don't know who's worse about trying to do more than she should, you or Samantha."

As Allie started to leave to put Irish Battleship away, Samantha came out of her office. "That was Cindy," she said. "She got a call from an old friend of hers in New York with some interesting news."

Allie felt her stomach knot. New York was where Gail Hickam lived. Had Cindy's friend found Allie's mother's cousin? She waited, afraid to hear what Samantha was about to say, but she couldn't walk away, either.

"It sounds like Legacy is for sale," Samantha said.

Allie felt a combination of relief and puzzlement.

"Is my dad going to buy him or give up his interest?" Parker asked.

Samantha shrugged. "I don't know about that," she said. "Cindy just called because she wanted me to tell you, Chris. The people in New York who bought out your interest in him are getting out of the business."

"Who is Legacy?" Allie asked.

"You know that Star was the last foal out of my mom's great racehorse, Ashleigh's Wonder, right?" Christina asked.

Allie nodded. "Wonder died after Star was born," she said.

"Right," Christina said. "Wonder's Legacy was born before Star. He was supposed to be her last foal, but then . . ." She wrinkled her face. "Mom gave her interest in Legacy to me, but I traded him for Sterling Dream a couple of years before Star was born."

Allie frowned. "But Samantha owns Sterling now," she said.

Christina nodded. "When I started working with Star, I couldn't give her the time she deserved."

"So I was lucky enough to get her for Whisperwood," Samantha interjected.

"Last year while we were at Belmont," Christina continued, "Cindy and I went to the farm where Legacy is living. He looked all right, but he didn't seem very happy." Christina made a sour face. "He never got a chance to prove himself on the track once he was sold." She sighed. "Maybe things would have been different for him if he'd stayed at Whitebrook. But I didn't want to be around racehorses back then. All I cared about was eventing. It took Star to change that."

Allie gazed at her, wondering if she would have done the same thing. "I'll bet you hurt your mom's feelings," she said, then clapped her hand over her mouth. "I'm sorry," she said quickly. "That was rude of me."

"Don't be sorry," Christina replied, grinning. "I really was a spoiled brat back then."

Allie couldn't believe Christina hadn't been grateful. She wished her biggest problem was having to pick one out of some of the greatest horses in racing. But she caught herself before she opened her mouth again.

Christina laughed. "Don't worry about being polite," she said. "I've grown up a lot in the last six years.

But really, I wasn't ready for a racehorse then, and I wasn't going to become a jockey just because Mom wanted me to. I had to make my own mistakes and choices and figure things out my own way."

Allie nodded in understanding.

"Unfortunately, Legacy lost out because of it," Christina added.

"How come Parker's dad has an interest in Legacy?" Allie asked.

"My grandfather gave Ashleigh a half interest in Wonder and all her foals," Parker explained. "Ashleigh saved Wonder's life, and that was his way of repaying her. I think my dad lost interest when Legacy's few performances on the track were less than spectacular," he said.

Samantha looked up at the clock on the wall and gasped. "You had better get Irish Battleship put away, Allie. The first class will be here any minute."

Allie led the mare away and quickly groomed her, giving her a handful of oats when she put her in her stall. "If I had to pick between you and one of the racehorses, I wonder which I'd choose," she said thoughtfully. But there wasn't much point in even wondering about that. *Stop thinking about it*, she ordered herself, then left Irish Battleship to go help Christina with the afternoon lessons.

"Remember," Christina told her when she dropped her off at Tall Oaks that evening, "if you have any questions, ask Cindy. She won't keep things from you, Allie. Cindy isn't like that."

Allie nodded. "I'll talk to her," she promised, climbing from the car. But she didn't really know how to bring it up, and she wondered why Cindy hadn't said anything about her mother's cousin.

When she walked into the cottage, Cindy was sitting on the sofa. She jumped up when Allie came into the room, a serious look on her face. She smiled, but Allie could see the strained look in her eyes, and her heart sank. Allie was sure that Cindy had bad news. The cousin was coming to get her, and she'd never see Tall Oaks, or all the people she was starting to care about, ever again.

"Go put your books away, and then we need to talk," Cindy said seriously.

Allie trudged to her room, then stood by her bed for a minute, looking at her parents' photograph. "I'll miss it here," she told them in a low voice. "It would be the perfect place to live if you were here with me."

Finally she returned to the living room, where Cindy was waiting for her.

"Okay," Allie said. "What is it?"

"I know you're doing a lot here," Cindy said, "between taking care of Image, helping with Jinx, helping out with the barn chores, and keeping your grades up."

Allie looked at her steadily, imagining her backbone as a steel rod. She could handle whatever it was, but Cindy didn't seem to be ready to tell her she was going to be taken away. "I'll do whatever I can," she said.

"I know," Cindy said. "But you need to do some fun things, too."

Allie shrugged. "The horses are fun," she said.

Cindy nodded. "True, but how about a change of scenery? I have to make a quick trip to New York on business. If you go with me, we could go to Aqueduct for some races, and do some sightseeing and shopping."

"New York?" Allie repeated warily. Was this Cindy's way of getting her together with Gail Hickam?

"You don't have to go," Cindy said, seeing Allie's reaction. "But I thought we could make a fun little trip out of it. We really haven't done a lot together, and it would be good for both of us."

Allie sighed. All she really could do was make the best of things. She couldn't complain about a weekend in New York, watching Thoroughbred racing and seeing some tourist attractions, could she? She looked at Cindy seriously. "I just don't want to be a problem for you," she said.

Cindy's jaw dropped. "A problem?" she repeated, shaking her head emphatically. She jumped up and wrapped her arms around Allie, giving her a warm hug. "You're far from a problem, sweetie." She held Allie at arm's length and looked at her intently. "You're the greatest kid in the world, and I'm lucky to have you here."

Allie felt all her fears fade with Cindy's words, and she hugged her foster mother in return. Cindy didn't seem to be worried about the social services people and Gail Hickam, Allie decided, so maybe she shouldn't let it bother her, either.

5

"A WEEKEND IN NEW YORK?" BRITTANY GAZED ACROSS THE cafeteria table at Allie. "Are you serious? I'd love to spend a weekend there. I'm jealous."

"Me too," Kendra said, taking a bite of her sandwich. "You're going to have a blast."

"I hope so," Allie said. She picked up a half of the French roll stuffed with lobster salad that Luis had packed for her. "Here, Roxanne," she said, holding the sandwich out. "As usual, I have too much lunch."

"I shouldn't," Roxanne said, then sighed and took the food. "But it tastes so good." She bit into the roll and groaned. "Better than good," she said through the mouthful of food. "It's heavenly."

Allie had been eating lunch every day with the same group, and although she was sure Kendra had told them about her parents, none of the other girls had asked any questions. She was grateful for their silent acceptance and found herself looking forward to getting together with them.

"When are you leaving?" Lila asked.

"Friday after school," Allie said, poking a melon ball with her fork. "We'll be back late Sunday evening."

"That's too bad," Abby said. "We're going to have a movie and pizza sleepover at Lila's on Saturday."

Lila nodded. "Maybe you'll be able to come to the next one we have," she said.

"I'd like that," Allie said, suddenly disappointed about her weekend plans. She knew that a sleepover wasn't nearly as exciting as a trip to New York, but it sounded like a lot of fun. Besides, she was still on edge about the possibility that this trip was really planned around a meeting with Gail Hickam, and Allie couldn't shake the thought that Cindy wasn't telling her everything about their reason for the trip.

When the warning bell rang for class, Lila walked to the lockers with Allie. "Maybe when you get back we can go riding," she suggested. "If you want to."

Allie shot her a surprised look. "I didn't know you rode," she said. "You never talk about horses. I wasn't even sure if you liked them or not."

Lila rolled her eyes. "I'm a politician's kid living in Horse Country, USA," she said. "We have three saddle horses at home. I'm probably not nearly as good as you are, but I haven't fallen off in years. Besides," she added, "I wasn't so sure you'd want to ride with me."

Allie raised her eyebrows. "*You* weren't sure?"

"Well," Lila said, leaning against the row of lockers, "you don't talk a lot about home, and I thought maybe you'd rather not talk about horses and stuff like that."

Allie laughed. "There's nothing else I'd rather talk about," she said. "Maybe you can come over to Tall Oaks. We have two saddle horses there, too, and lots of trails. I'll ask Cindy if it's okay."

Lila smiled. "I'd like to do that," she said, pushing away from the locker. "I'd better get to class. See you later."

As Lila headed down the hall, Allie grabbed her own books from her locker and hurried to her fourth-period class. She was excited about the idea of going riding with Lila when she got back from New York. Riding with Melanie on the track was great, and Kevin had gone trail riding with her on the Arabian saddle horses Ben and Cindy owned, but she'd really like to have a friend the same age to do horse things with. She hoped Cindy wouldn't mind that she had invited Lila to the farm.

The week passed quickly. Now that Allie knew Lila had horses, the talk at lunch revolved around riding. Allie learned that both Kendra and Brittany owned Dutch warmbloods, and Roxanne took lessons at a nearby stable. Abby's uncle trained racehorses, and she often visited the farm where he worked, and helped out with the yearlings.

"Riding a filly out of Miss Battleship and by Finn McCoul? How lucky is that?" Kendra asked when Allie told them about riding Irish Battleship at Whisperwood. "And getting private lessons from Parker Townsend? He's awesome."

"And cute, too," Lila added.

"He and Christina make a great couple," Allie said.

"It must be so cool to ride with Melanie and Christina," Abby said. "Think of what you can learn from two jockeys who've won Triple Crown races."

"It seems like it would be hard to be around race-horses after your dad . . ." Brittany's voice trailed off, and she bit her lower lip. "I'm sorry, Allie," she said quickly. "I didn't mean to—"

"It's okay," Allie reassured her with a smile. But she was relieved when lunch ended. She loved horses and riding, but the ache she felt every time she thought about her father was still deep.

Allie was so busy with her work at Whisperwood, helping with the horses at Tall Oaks, and keeping up with her homework that the week sped by. But Friday afternoon she found herself worrying again about the real reason Cindy had suggested a trip to New York. She walked out of the school with Kendra and Lila to see Cindy standing by a dark blue sedan that was parked near the buses.

"I'll see you two on Monday," she told the other girls.

"Have fun!" both girls called as Allie hurried over to the car.

"Everything's packed, and we're all set to go," Cindy announced. She gestured for Allie to climb into the back of the car, while Cindy slid into the front passenger seat. The driver, a short, gray-haired man Allie had never seen before, eyed her from the rearview mirror.

"All buckled up, miss?" he asked before putting the car in gear.

"Yes, sir," she said politely, then winced inwardly. Was she supposed to call a chauffeur "sir"?

"My name is Rich," he said, his blue eyes crinkling into a mass of wrinkles as he smiled.

"I'm Allie," she replied. A shout from outside the car drew her attention to the sidewalk, where Lila and Kendra were waving at her. Allie waved back as Rich pulled around the buses and onto the road.

"Who was that?" Cindy asked, turning in her seat to glance at Allie.

"My friends," Allie told her. Cindy's expression turned serious, but then she nodded and smiled. "I'm glad you're making friends," she said. "It's important."

"They're nice," Allie said, then settled back on the seat. Why would Cindy look so concerned if she was happy that Allie had friends at school? *Unless she doesn't want me to get too close to any of the kids here*, she answered herself silently, and sank back against the leather upholstery. She should have stuck to her plan not to make friends. It was going to make it that much harder to leave.

When they arrived at the airport in Keeneland, Rich dropped them off at the terminal, pulling their travel bags from the trunk of the car. "I'll be waiting for you and Miss Allie when your flight comes in on Sunday," he informed Cindy as he handed them their bags.

"We'll see you then," Cindy said, picking up her suitcase. Allie did the same, and they went through the security gates and checked their bags.

Allie had the window seat on the plane, and as they took off she stared down at the Kentucky countryside dropping away beneath them, until the fenced fields and rooftops of the buildings disappeared beneath the clouds.

"Is there anything you'd especially like to see this weekend?" Cindy asked, unbuckling her seatbelt.

Allie looked at Cindy and shrugged. "I'd like to see the American Museum of Natural History," she said. "I have to write a report for class, and I thought I could get some good information at the museum."

Cindy raised her eyebrows and gave Allie a long look. "Are you always this studious?" she asked.

Allie glanced down at her hands. "Not always," she said. "But it just seemed practical."

Cindy chuckled, then reached over and patted Allie's hand. "We can visit the museum," she said. "I lived in New York for twelve years, and I never thought about going there. It'll be a good experience for me, too." She pulled a couple of magazines out of her purse and offered one to Allie. "I found a great article about Meadow Star in this one. I thought you'd like to read about Alpine Meadow's dam."

Allie took the magazine and flipped through it until she found the article Cindy had mentioned. As she read Meadow Star's story, she began to understand why Cindy had wanted Alpine Meadow. When she finished reading, she turned to Cindy, who was looking over some papers that looked like legal documents.

Cindy looked up at Allie and smiled, then folded the papers and stuffed them into her bag. "Good article, huh? Meadow Star's owner knew she was going to be an awesome racehorse, and he donated all her winnings to the Children's Rescue Fund."

Allie nodded. "I read that Meadow Star's purses raised almost a million dollars for the fund," she said. "I can see why you wanted to have one of her foals."

Cindy nodded. "When I was racing, I always donated part of my winnings to the CRF. I could never have contributed as much as Meadow Star did, but it was important to me to do something. And now, with Ben's help, I have Alpine Meadow. We agreed that if she turns out to be a solid runner, we're going to use her winnings to help kids."

Allie nodded thoughtfully. "I like that idea," she said. "I'll help with her any way I can."

When the plane touched down in New York, Cindy and Allie disembarked with the rest of the passengers and waited at the luggage pickup for their bags. Cindy gazed around, taking in the crowd of people rushing about the terminal. "I always forget how busy this place gets until I come back," she said.

"Do you miss living here?" Allie asked, watching a young couple with a baby greet a middle-aged man and woman, who immediately began fussing over the infant. Several people in suits strode past, raincoats flung over their arms, swinging briefcases and umbrellas, moving purposefully toward the exits.

"Here's your suitcase," Cindy said, holding up Allie's plain black bag.

"How can you tell it from the rest?" Allie asked, staring at the carousel loaded with baggage.

"I put a Tall Oaks sticker on it," Cindy said, turning the case so that Allie could see the bright green label with purple lettering. "I had them printed up a few weeks ago, just for fun."

"Cool," Allie said, picking up her bag. "Did you put one on yours, too?"

"Of course," Cindy replied, snagging her own suitcase from the conveyer. She held it up. "Matching cases," she told Allie, laughing.

Soon they were in a taxi, heading for a motel near the Aqueduct racetrack. "We'll get our stuff put away and then go out for dinner," Cindy told Allie. "Then we can go over to Rockefeller Center. Have you ever ice-skated?"

"No," Allie said. "I used to have some in-line skates, and my friends and I back home . . ." She let her voice trail off, thinking about the fun she had had with her friends back in California.

"I know it's still hard for you," Cindy said. She exhaled heavily. "For a long time after my folks died, I was really angry at them for leaving me alone. I know your parents loved you very much, and you still miss them."

Allie stared down at her lap, nodding slowly. "All the time," she said quietly.

"I wish I could make the hurt just go away for you," Cindy said. "I don't feel like I'm doing a good job taking care of you."

Allie sucked in her breath. This was it. Cindy had decided she didn't have time to be a foster parent, and she was going to tell her about Gail. Allie braced herself for the bad news.

"I felt horrible today when I saw your friends waving goodbye to you and I didn't even know about them." Cindy shook her head, looking disgusted. "I get so wrapped up with the horses that I forget some of the things I should be doing, like paying more attention to you."

Allie felt Cindy shift her weight, and she looked up slowly to see Cindy eyeing her anxiously. "You're going to have to be patient with me," Cindy said softly. "I was lucky enough to have Ian and Beth take me in, so I know how it feels to have good, loving parents. I just don't have any experience being one."

Allie released her pent-up breath and stared at Cindy. "You're doing great," she said. "I really am happy at Tall Oaks, even if I don't act like it all the time."

Cindy stared at her. "You've got the best attitude in

the world!" she exclaimed. "I think I'm really lucky to be able to share my home with you, and everyone at Whitebrook and Whisperwood loves you, too."

The driver stopped the cab in front of the motel, and before long they were in their room. Allie felt much better after what Cindy had said. Cindy seemed to be as worried about making things work as Allie was. She set her suitcase at the foot of her bed and turned to Cindy. "I really meant it," she said, feeling very adult. "You're a great foster parent."

Cindy smiled, looking relieved. "Thanks," she replied. "But you're going to have to help me with the parenting part." She wrinkled her nose. "I can take criticism, you know. Not very gracefully, but I can take it."

"Me too," Allie said, and they both laughed.

"Good." Cindy propped her fists on her hips and looked Allie in the eyes. "Now that that's settled, let's go get some food."

They had pizza in a little restaurant that Cindy said she had eaten at often when she was a jockey. "When I was starting out, good, cheap food was important," she told Allie. "I could make a week's worth of dinners from one pizza."

Allie curled her lip, setting down her slice of pepperoni pizza. "Week-old pizza?" she asked. "That sounds terrible."

Cindy chuckled. "Now you know why Luis keeps sending food down to the cottage," she said.

Allie nodded. "I know all the girls I eat lunch with are completely jealous of the lunch he packs for me," she said.

Cindy leaned back against the booth they were sitting in. "Tell me about your friends," she encouraged, and for the next hour, Allie told Cindy about her teachers, her new friends, and her classes, and Cindy listened intently.

"I think it would be a great idea to have Lila come over," she said. "And maybe you could invite the whole bunch to Tall Oaks for a sleepover sometime." She grinned. "I'll bet we could even talk Luis into preparing one of his incredible meals for you."

After dinner in Manhattan they walked to Rockefeller Center and watched the skaters glide around the ice, some with grace and skill, others wobbling around the edges of the big rink, clinging to each other, and falling down.

"Do you want to try it?" Cindy asked.

Allie shook her head. "I'm afraid I'd break my ankle and not be able to ride for a while," she confessed.

Cindy nodded. "That was always my feeling, too," she said. "I never wanted to risk not being able to ride."

"Did you ever want to do cross-country or show jumping?" Allie asked.

Cindy shook her head. "Once I got around the horses at Whitebrook, I knew I had to be a jockey. There was no question about it."

Allie watched a young girl spin in a dizzying circle on the ice, her arms outflung and her head tilted back. "I think I want to race, too," she said. "But most of the girls at school are into eventing, and I do like jumping."

"Sammy says you have great potential as an eventing competitor," Cindy said. "It's nice that you have a chance to try both racing and jumping so you can decide which you love to do most."

Allie nodded. Her parents had encouraged her to work with eventing horses, even though their lives revolved around the racetrack. She'd rather exercise the racehorses than work in the arena, but she wondered if she should do what her mom and dad had wanted.

Would they have been upset with her if she chose to follow in their footsteps? She'd never know. The thought left her with that miserable, lost feeling that always seemed to be hovering around her, and suddenly the evening didn't seem so fun.

"If you don't mind, I'd like to go back to the motel and go to bed," she said to Cindy.

Cindy nodded. "We can go over to the track early tomorrow and check out the barns," she said. "If you'd like to, that is."

Allie nodded agreeably. "I'd like that," she said. The idea of wandering through the Aqueduct stables with Cindy, looking at all those magnificent Thoroughbreds, sounded much more interesting than standing there in the dark watching the skaters.

Cindy grinned broadly. "A girl after my own heart," she said. "Let's get out of here." They found a taxi and rode back to the motel in Queens.

In spite of the empty feeling that always seemed to be hovering over her, the time she and Cindy had spent talking made her feel closer to her foster mother. For the first time since her father's death, she slept well, without the dreams of her parents that always left her feeling despondent when she awoke.

The next morning they arrived at the track while dawn was just breaking. Because of Cindy's credentials, they were able to go in through the back gate, and they spent some time strolling through the shed rows.

"Cindy, is that you?" A slim, dark-haired woman came out of a stall as Allie and Cindy walked through the barn.

"Rachel!" Cindy exclaimed. "I was hoping you'd be here."

Rachel gave Allie a curious look. "Who's your friend?" she asked Cindy.

"Rachel, I'd like you to meet Allie Avery," she said. "Allie, this is Rachel McGrady. Rachel and her husband, Matt, were my first friends when I moved to New York."

Rachel was looking intently at Allie. "You look familiar," she said. "Have I met you before?"

"Allie moved to Kentucky last fall from California," Cindy explained.

Rachel's eyes widened. "You're Craig Avery's daughter," she said. "We were so sorry to hear about your mom and dad."

Allie nodded silently, not sure how to respond.

"Allie's living with me now," Cindy told Rachel.

She glanced into the stall Rachel had come out of. "Who is this?" she asked.

Grateful to Cindy for changing the subject, Allie peered into the stall to see a tall bay filly, a crooked blaze marking her elegant head.

"This is Matt's latest wonder horse, Trillium," Rachel told them. "She's running in the Corrections Stakes this afternoon."

"She's beautiful," Allie said, holding her hand out so that the filly could sniff her palm. The bay nuzzled her palm, popping her lips as she searched for a treat.

"She likes you," Rachel said, folding her arms in front of her and leaning against the wall.

"I like her, too," Allie replied, running her hand along the filly's smooth nose.

"We'll be here to watch her run," Cindy told Rachel. "I have a quick business meeting a little later, but we'll be back at the track for the afternoon program." She looked around curiously. "Is Matt here?" she asked. "I haven't seen him in ages."

Rachel shook her head. "He's down in Florida this week," she said. "I'm it for the McGrady barn."

Trillium nudged Allie's hand, demanding more attention, and Allie absently stroked the filly's neck.

"If you don't want to sit through some dull meeting with Cindy, you could hang out here this morning and help me with her," Rachel offered.

To Allie's dismay, Cindy looked relieved. "That's a great idea," she said quickly.

Allie felt as though she'd been dismissed, and she turned away from Cindy to pet Trillium. "That would be fine," she said, her good mood from their talk the night before fading.

"We're going to check out more horses, then go have breakfast at the track kitchen," Cindy told Rachel.

"Sounds good," Rachel said, smiling at Allie. "I'll see you later, okay?"

Allie nodded, petting the filly one last time, then followed Cindy in silence through the backside, stopping when Cindy did to talk to several more trainers and jockeys she knew. Allie went through the motions of being polite, interested, and cheerful, but all the while she was worried about Cindy's unexplained business meeting, and the renewed concern about her own future dampened her mood for the rest of the morning.

6

"I'LL BE BACK IN A COUPLE OF HOURS," CINDY INFORMED Allie when they returned to the McGradys' stable area.

"I could go with you," Allie offered. She wouldn't mind staying at the track with Rachel if only she knew what Cindy's meeting was about. But she had a strong feeling that Cindy was keeping something from her, and the only thing she could imagine was that it was about Gail Hickam.

"Oh, I think you'd be bored to tears," Cindy said quickly. "I'll be back in time to watch the races with you."

Rachel, who was standing by Trillium's stall, nod-ded. "We'll be fine here," she said.

The bay filly had her head poked over the door, and Cindy gave her nose a pat. "We'll see you later, then," she said, and walked away.

Allie watched Cindy go, suddenly gripped with the urge to chase after her. She reached over to run her hand along Trillium's neck, drawing comfort from the feel of the filly's warm, sleek coat.

Rachel draped her arm over Allie's shoulders and gave her a squeeze. "If you'd like, you can help me get Trillium ready for her race. There's plenty to do."

Allie nodded silently. At least she'd be busy with the horse while she was waiting for Cindy's return. *Quit acting like a little ninny*, she scolded herself. *There's nothing you can do about any of this.* The thought depressed her. She hated feeling as though so many other people had control of her future.

"Let's take our girl over to the wash rack," Rachel said, holding Trillium's lead out to Allie. "We'll make her look fabulous for her race, okay?"

"Sure," Allie said, clipping the lead onto the filly's halter.

"I'm glad you came up with Cindy for the weekend," Rachel told her as they walked Trillium to the end of the shed row. "How do you like living at Tall Oaks?"

"It's nice there," Allie said. "I hope I get to stay."

Rachel gave her a look of surprise. "Why wouldn't you?" she asked, stopping at the wash rack.

Allie tied Trillium to the cross ties. "Because social services is looking for my relatives," she said.

Rachel frowned. "Cindy didn't say anything about that," she said. "I'm sure if there was a problem, she'd talk to you about it."

Allie shrugged. "I guess so," she said.

"I know so," Rachel replied emphatically, running warm water over Trillium's back. "I've known Cindy a long time, and she'd never keep something as serious as that a secret." She handed Allie a bottle of shampoo. "Cindy went through a lot when she lost her own parents, and I know she wants you to have the best, happiest home possible."

Allie squirted shampoo onto a soft sponge and began working the lather into the filly's coat, mulling over Rachel's words. If the social services people decided that the best place for her was with her mom's cousin, there wasn't a lot Cindy could do about that. She forced the bleak thought from her mind and focused on Trillium.

The bay filly closed her eyes and dropped her head,

allowing Allie to massage her neck with the soapy sponge. "You're a sweetie," Allie murmured, working the soap into her coat. When she finished, Rachel hosed the shampoo from Trillium's coat and helped Allie dry the filly, then draped a sheet over her.

Around them, other grooms were walking horses, and Allie admired the graceful Thoroughbreds, with their long, slender legs and muscled builds. *This is what I want to do,* she thought. *I want to be around race-horses.* She thought about what Beckie had said, that she looked forward to the things that reminded her of her grandmother. *Maybe in time I'll get to that point when I think of Dad and Mom,* she thought. *Maybe I really will become a jockey.*

As they walked Trillium back to her stall a slender young man came out of the barn office, a set of silks draped over his arm. "Hey, Rachel," he called, waving. "I see you've hired a new groom."

"Hi, Kenny," Rachel said, then turned to Allie. "Allie Avery, this is Kenny Potts, Trillium's jockey this afternoon."

Kenny extended his hand, and Allie shook it. "I'm pleased to meet you," she said. "But I'm not an official groom, just a guest horse washer."

Kenny laughed, the friendly sound brightening Allie's mood. In spite of her worries, she smiled back

Kenny patted Trillium's neck. "She looks great," he said. "I'll be proud to take her onto the track this afternoon."

"Thanks," Allie said, then turned to Rachel. "I'll brush out her mane and tail and wrap her legs if you want me to."

"That would be great," Rachel said. "But don't feel like you have to work."

"It isn't work," Allie said. "I love to groom."

"I've got a couple of other trainers I need to meet with before the races," Kenny said. "Any last-minute instructions?"

"Not a thing," Rachel said. "You know how to handle her. Matt and I have all the confidence in the world in you. We'll see you at the viewing paddock."

Before long, Allie had Trillium groomed and ready for her race. She sat outside the filly's stall and waited anxiously for Cindy to return. The time seemed to drag, but finally she spotted a familiar figure coming up the aisle, and she jumped to her feet.

Cindy grinned broadly, and Allie felt a rush of relief. Whatever Cindy's meeting had been about, it had apparently gone well for her to look so pleased. Which, Allie figured, was good news for her.

"Shall we go find a good spot at the grandstand?" Cindy asked.

Rachel stepped out of her office. "Can Allie come back before Trillium's race?" she asked. "Since she did such a knockout job grooming Trillium, I thought she might like to stand in as her handler for the race."

"I'd love to!" Allie exclaimed.

"Let's go get some lunch and watch the first few races," Cindy said. "You can come back and help Rachel after that."

Soon Allie and Cindy were settled near the finish line, waiting for the first of the post parades.

"I like that gray colt," Allie said, pointing at the third horse prancing along the track.

Cindy nodded. "I think that big chestnut looks pretty good," she said, pointing at the sixth horse.

"I'll stick with number three," Allie said, moving to the rail so that she could watch the horses closely. Cindy joined her, and when the race started, they cheered their favorites on. When Allie's gray colt crossed the finish line first, she pumped her fist in the air. "Woo-hoo!" she exclaimed. "I picked the winner!"

Cindy laughed. "My colt didn't do too badly," she said. "Second to last isn't as slow as last."

Allie looked at the program, running her finger along the list of jockeys. "Trillium's jockey is riding in the next race," she said, then watched closely as the horses were led from the viewing ring onto the track. Kenny was riding the number five horse. Allie watched the big black colt buck and prance, fighting the pony horse as they passed in front of the grandstand.

"He looks like a problem horse," she told Cindy. "I hope Kenny gets him settled fast."

Cindy nodded, eyeing the fractious colt. "He does look like a handful," she agreed.

Allie could see the grim expression on Kenny's face as he struggled to keep the colt in line. The pony rider had the big black's lead line pulled short, keeping the colt crowded against the stocky quarter horse he rode. As they passed from view, moving into line behind the starting gate, Allie strained to keep track of Kenny and his mount, but the tote board blocked her view.

After several minutes she shifted her weight impatiently. "It sure is taking them a long time to start the race," she said, gazing at the empty track.

"They're probably having a problem loading a horse," Cindy said, drumming her fingers on the rail.

Suddenly a riderless horse galloped into view, racing wildly along the backside. Allie gave a cry of horror. "That's Kenny's horse!" she exclaimed, pressing her hands to her mouth, feeling her heart pounding in her chest.

"Oh, no," Cindy gasped as the track ambulance sped onto the track, heading for the starting gate. She reached over and put her arm around Allie. "It's probably nothing," she said.

But Allie knew better. She stood frozen, watching the outrider chase down the runaway horse, but her thoughts were on Kenny. She couldn't block out the memory of what had happened to her father. "We need to find out if he's okay," she said to Cindy, trembling with anxiety. The thought she'd had earlier of working with racehorses as a full-time job came back to haunt her. What had she been thinking?

The outrider caught the colt and headed for the backside with the excited black in tow as the ambulance drove off the track.

"Let's get over to the infirmary," Cindy said, taking Allie by the hand and hurrying away from the track.

All the way to the backside, Allie's mind raced with a jumble of thoughts—about her father, about how risky being a jockey could be, and about her own passion for horses. Why did it have to be so dangerous? She felt herself starting to get angry. It wasn't fair.

When they reached the building that housed the track's medical facility, Allie hesitated at the door. "What if he isn't okay?" she asked Cindy. "What if . . ." Her voice trailed off.

Cindy gave her a hug. "I'm sure he's all right," she reassured Allie, then led her into the waiting area.

The room was empty. Allie stared at the closed door that led into the exam area, willing it to open.

Finally a man in a white jacket stepped into the lobby. "Are you Mr. Potts's family?" he asked.

"We're friends," Cindy said quickly. "Is he all right?"

The doctor smiled and nodded. "You can go see him," he said. "He's going to be fine." He held the door and gestured for them to follow him. He stopped at an open doorway and poked his head inside. "You have visitors," he announced, then stepped back to let Cindy and Allie through.

Kenny was sitting on the edge of the table, a white bandage covering the side of his jaw.

Her relief at seeing Kenny all right overwhelmed Allie, and she felt herself start to tremble all over again.

Kenny twisted the unbandaged side of his face into a crooked smile. "I'm fine," he told her. "I hear the colt is okay, too."

"That's good," Cindy said. "What happened?"

Kenny rolled his eyes. "When they got him halfway into the gate, he went straight up, hit his head, then really panicked and flipped over backward." He touched the bandage. "I bumped my chin on the gate while I was bailing off," he said. "It isn't bad, but I'll have a great bruise to remember it by." His eyes twinkled. "And I'm good to go for Trillium's race," he added. "They just wanted me here to make sure I didn't have a concussion."

"You're still going to race?" Allie asked.

"Of course," Kenny said, sounding surprised. "What's the number one rule about falling off a horse?"

Allie grimaced. For a moment she wondered if Kenny was downplaying the accident at the gate to make her feel better, but then she saw that he was just being realistic. Part of a jockey's life was the risk of getting injured, and if you were going to succeed in the sport, you had to accept that. Both her parents had loved racing enough to take the chance. Allie thought back to when she was younger, and the thrill and pride she always felt at seeing one of them racing. She would never have asked either of them to stop riding, although if she had, she was certain her father would have walked away from the track in a second.

"When you fall off, you get right back on," she said to Kenny.

"And that's what I'm going to do," Kenny said. "I can't let a little mishap stop me."

Cindy nodded in agreement. "We'll be watching you on the track," she said, then turned to Allie. "Let's go see Rachel so you can help her with Trillium."

Rachel was waiting for them, Trillium's tack sitting by her stall. While Cindy watched, Allie helped Rachel do a final grooming on the filly.

"She's ready," Rachel said, stepping back to look the horse over.

"She looks excellent," Cindy said. "I'm going to the track, but I'll be close to the winner's circle."

She headed back to the grandstand, and Allie led Trillium toward the viewing ring. The filly had her head up, and she pranced a little as they entered the saddling area.

"You're excited, aren't you?" Allie asked her, patting the alert filly's neck. Trillium snorted, testing the air as the other horses gathered in the saddling ring. Rachel brought the tack over, and Allie draped the number four blanket over Trillium's back, then buckled the lightweight racing saddle in place.

"It looks like you have things under control," Rachel said. "I'll see you in a few minutes." She went into the viewing paddock, standing at the number four spot with a tall, gray-haired man dressed in a dark blue suit. His tie matched Kenny's silks, and Allie knew he must be Trillium's owner.

Allie joined the other handlers, walking Trillium around the viewing ring so that the fans could see the horses close up. She saw Kenny walk into the ring to stand beside Rachel and the filly's owner. Kenny had taken the bandage off, and she could see that the cut on his jaw was as minor as he had claimed.

She stopped Trillium in front of Kenny, and Rachel boosted him onto the filly's back. The owner gave Allie a pleasant smile and an approving nod. Allie smiled back, then walked the filly over to the entrance to the track to hand her off to one of the waiting pony riders. "Good luck," she told Kenny, who gave her a broad grin and a thumbs-up.

"Trillium's a great ride," he said, buckling his helmet into place. "I've got all the luck I need just being on her."

He rode off, and Allie returned to Rachel, who introduced her to Trillium's owner, Bob Thuring. "You look pretty confident around the racehorses for such a young person," Mr. Thuring said. "I'm glad Rachel had you handle my filly." He turned to Rachel. "I'll be up in the grandstand. But," he added with a grin, "with the way Trillium looks, I'm sure I'll be meeting you at the winner's circle." He glanced back at Allie. "That includes you, young lady."

Allie and Rachel left the horse's owner and walked to the area in front of the grandstand, where Cindy was on her cell phone.

"Everything went perfectly," she was saying. "Smooth as silk, Ben, and the whole deal isn't even going to cost as much as we thought." She glanced up as Allie reached her. "Anyway, the race is about to start, so I guess we can finish talking about this when we get home." She ended the call and tucked her phone back into her purse.

"Trillium and Kenny look good," she said to Rachel as the horses paraded past them. Trillium was cantering beside the pony horse, keeping her pace even with the other horse's extended trot. "This is going to be a good race."

Allie waited tensely, gripping the rail so tightly that her hands ached, bracing herself for another disaster at the gate. She wondered fleetingly about the deal Cindy had been talking about , but she was so worried about the potential for another disaster on the track that she forgot about Cindy's phone call.

Moments after the horses were loaded, the starting bell rang, and she strained to spot Kenny and Trillium in the pack of racehorses as they flew down the far side of the track.

"Look!" Cindy said, pointing at the front edge of the field. "Kenny's got her on the outside, coming up on the two leaders."

Allie found the bay and held her breath as they galloped into the curve. Kenny was keeping Trillium rated, holding her back enough that she would have something left for the end of the race.

"He's riding smart," Cindy commented as the horses came out of the turn and onto the straight stretch.

Allie watched him lean forward slightly, moving his hands far up on the filly's neck, and Trillium responded by switching gears. The two lead horses were running strongly, but Trillium blew past them in a flash, charging down the final stretch, leaving a huge gap between herself and the other horses.

"It's no contest," the announcer shouted. "Trillium is ahead by five—no, six, *seven* lengths. Trillium is the clear winner of the Corrections Stakes!"

Allie jumped up and down, clapping her hands. "We won," she cried excitedly. "Kenny and Trillium won!"

"Let's go get her," Rachel said, catching Allie by the elbow. "Time for the winner's circle."

Allie followed Rachel onto the track, meeting Kenny and Trillium near the opening into the winner's circle. Kenny's smile was bright, his eyes sparkling. "That sure made up for the second race," he said, hopping off the filly's back as Allie clipped the lead to her headstall. He quickly stripped the saddle and stepped onto the scales so that the clerk could check his weight.

Allie held Trillium proudly as Kenny hopped back onto the filly and stood beside Mr. Thuring and Rachel as the official photographer took pictures. Then she led the filly to the vet barn, where the top three finishers in each race were tested for drugs.

"I'll take care of this," Rachel offered when they reached the vet barn. "You did a great job. Anytime you want to work up here, just let me know. I can keep you busy for days on end."

"Thanks," Allie said. She left the barn to find Cindy.

"Let's go do some of those sightseeing things you had in mind," Cindy told her.

They spent the afternoon and evening visiting the American Museum of Natural History, catching the ferry out into the harbor to see the Statue of Liberty, and then having dinner at a nice restaurant downtown. By the time they returned to the motel, Allie was exhausted.

"The museum was amazing and the Statue of Liberty is awesome, but the best part of the day was seeing Trillium win the race," she told Cindy when she came out of the bathroom in her pajamas.

Cindy was already in bed, looking over those mysterious papers she had been reading on the plane. She glanced up at Allie and smiled warmly. "I'm so glad you feel that way," she said. "I was pretty excited for Rachel and Matt, too. Maybe when we get home," she added, "you can start doing more with the racehorses at Tall Oaks. I'd appreciate it if you'd help me start Alpine Meadow. She's ready to be backed."

"I'd like that," Allie said. She had never helped get a young racehorse used to the weight of a rider, but she had watched it done so many times that she knew exactly what to do.

"The problem would be that you wouldn't have as much time to spend at Whisperwood," Cindy said. "You'll have to think about what you want to do most."

Allie nodded. She wanted to ride with Lila, and she liked jumping, but even after the terrifying moment when she had thought Kenny might be badly hurt, she still loved the track and the racehorses more than anything.

7

WHEN CINDY AND ALLIE RETURNED TO TALL OAKS ON
Sunday evening, Allie stared out the window at the
farm as Rich guided the sedan up the long, curved
drive. The ancient oak trees that lined the driveway
were bare, pointing spindly branches toward the dark-
ening sky. But lights shone from the mansion on the
hill, and when they rolled to a stop at Cindy's cottage,
Allie saw that someone had turned the lights on in the
little house. It all looked safe and homey, and Allie
breathed a little prayer that she would be able to stay
there for a long time.

Rich stopped in front of the cottage. "Here you go,

ladies," he said, climbing from the car and opening the door for Allie.

"Home sweet home," Cindy said, opening her own door. She turned to look at Allie. "Are you ready to get back into the school and work routine after your wild weekend in the big city?"

Allie nodded, slipping out of the car. Rich pulled their suitcases out of the trunk and carried them up to the house.

"I had fun in New York," she told Cindy. "But I'm glad to be back here." She gazed toward the barn. "After I put my stuff away, I want to go see Alpine Meadow, Jinx, and Image."

"You can do that first," Cindy told her as they followed Rich up the walk. "There isn't much to unpack. I'll have Rich put your bag in your room, and you can sort out your laundry and souvenirs later."

"Thanks," Allie said over her shoulder as she hurried toward the barn, eager to see the horses.

Beckie was closing the feed-room door when Allie walked into the big building. "Welcome home," the groom greeted her. "Did you have a good trip?"

Allie quickly filled her in on the weekend. "How was Jinx?" she asked.

"Awful, as usual," Beckie said, shaking her head in disgust. "I'm sure now that you're back he'll be good as gold. Melanie spent a lot of time here while you were gone, since it seems no one but the two of you can manage him."

"Is there anything I can help you with here?" Allie asked.

Beckie shook her head. "I'm just putting away the last of the feed cans," she said. "Everything else is done for the evening."

"Then I'm going to go visit the horses," Allie said.

"I'm heading home," the groom said. "I'll see you tomorrow morning."

Beckie left the barn, and Allie walked down the aisle, stopping when she got to Alpine Meadow. "I know why Cindy likes you so much," she told the filly. "I'm going to help you become a world-class racehorse so you can raise money to help orphans, just like your dam."

Alpine nudged Allie's shoulder, demanding affection, and Allie spent a few minutes petting the sociable filly before she moved on. When she reached Image's stall, the big black filly nickered, then tossed her head impatiently.

"I know," Allie said. "You thought I'd deserted you, but I'm here, girl." She checked the support wraps on Image's leg, then ran her hand along the filly's shoulder. "You're doing really well," she said, then threw her arms around Image's neck and buried her nose in the filly's mane, inhaling deeply. The sweet scent of Image's warm coat filled her with a feeling of contentment, and she heaved a sigh. "I'm so glad Melanie worked so hard to save you," she told Image. "Now I'm going to go visit Jinx, then I have to go back to the house."

She went into the stallion barn, pausing at Wonder's Champion's stall. The big chestnut horse eyed her, and Allie put her hand out to let him sniff her palm. "Cindy was so lucky the way everything worked out for her," she said, running her fingers along his silky soft nose. "Maybe someday I'll be lucky enough to have my own fantastic Thoroughbred."

She heard a loud banging farther down the barn and hurried toward it, past Khan's stall, to where she could see Jinx's copper-colored head sticking into the aisle. The colt squealed when he saw her, slamming his leg into the stall door.

"Stop that!" she exclaimed, shaking her finger at

him. Jinx raised his head and released a loud snort. "You are a big brat," Allie told the colt, stopping in front of his stall. Jinx tossed his head defiantly and banged the stall door again.

"Are you giving me what-for because I was gone all weekend?" she asked, propping her fists on her hips.

Jinx nickered low in his throat, thrusting his head over the stall door. Allie patted his nose. "You really did miss me, didn't you?" she asked. In response, Jinx shoved his head into her chest, and Allie pushed it back. "You need to mind your manners," she said sternly. "I missed you, too, but can't I leave for a couple of days without you getting an attitude?"

Jinx angled his head and snorted again.

Allie shook her head. "I guess not," she said. She felt a gentle bump against her leg and looked down to see Riley staring up at her, his paw resting on her shin. "I'm glad to see you, too," she said, squatting down to cradle the dog's head in her hands. Riley licked her chin, making Allie giggle. "I wish your good manners would rub off on Jinx," she told him, then rose to give the colt another caress.

"The only thing that would make Tall Oaks better would be if I had a horse of my own," she said, looking around at all the empty stalls. Coming out to the barn to visit her own horse would be wonderful. She sighed and turned back to Jinx. "I'm going back to the house," she told the animals. Riley flopped to the floor in front of Jinx's stall and looked up at her, wrinkling his forehead as he pricked up his floppy ears, then thumped his tail. Jinx hung his head over the stall door, standing guard over his little companion, making Allie smile. "I'll see you two first thing in the morning."

Allie strolled back up to the house, inhaling the fresh, cold air. New York had been exciting to visit and Aqueduct had been nice, but it really was good to be back in Kentucky.

She entered the cottage by the kitchen door and caught a whiff of spicy-smelling food. Her stomach rumbled, and she took another deep breath, trying to identify the aroma. It didn't matter. If whatever it was tasted half as good as it smelled, it would be delicious, and she was starving. She hurried out of the kitchen, intent on getting her things put away and washing up for dinner.

When she came into the living room, Ben and Cindy were leaning over Cindy's desk, reviewing some documents.

"Have you discussed this with Allie?" Ben was saying. "She may not like the idea, Cindy. This decision should include her."

"I was waiting until after the meeting," Cindy said. "I didn't know if this deal would go through. And," she added, "before I did anything, I wanted to go over this with you and make sure all the legalities were taken care of. But even if she isn't interested, it's still the right thing to do."

"How much time do we have?" Ben asked.

"Maybe a couple of weeks," Cindy said. "I'll get confirmation tomorrow. Meanwhile we have to sit tight and hope everything works out the way we want."

Allie froze in the doorway. What legalities? Whatever it was, it involved her. What was going on?

Cindy glanced over her shoulder, and when she saw Allie, she quickly tucked the papers back into their manila envelope. "How are the horses?" she asked.

"They were glad to see me," Allie said, staying where she was.

"Did you enjoy New York?" Ben inquired. "Luis missed having you to cook for."

"It looks like he made up for it," Cindy said, chuckling. "Did you smell that chicken casserole that's in the oven?"

Allie nodded, while Ben laughed. "I'd hardly call his chicken Italiana a casserole," he said.

"If you want to wash up, I'll get the table set," Cindy told Allie. Then she looked at Ben and wrinkled her nose. "I'll dish us up some of that yummy casserole, okay?"

Allie hurried from the room as Ben burst out laughing. Once she was in her room, she sank onto the edge of the bed. She wished she knew what was going on. But from the way Cindy had been acting, even if Allie asked, Cindy would probably avoid telling her. She gazed at the photo of her parents on the nightstand.

"What should I do?" she asked, frustration building inside her. Both Christina and Rachel, who knew Cindy well, had assured her that Cindy wouldn't do anything that might hurt Allie, and if there was something going on that could affect her staying at Tall Oaks, Cindy would tell her. So what was the big secret that Cindy was keeping?

Allie opened her suitcase and pulled out her dirty clothes, stuffing them into the hamper, then took the

New York souvenirs she had bought with the money she'd earned working at Whisperwood and laid them on the bed. She had bought herself a statue of a running Thoroughbred with Aqueduct's name printed on the base, and a poster of a chestnut Thoroughbred posed in a field of wildflowers. When she had seen it, she had instantly imagined herself there, walking across the colorful field to her own waiting Thoroughbred.

She looked around the room, trying to decide which wall to hang the print on. But the walls were already covered with framed artwork, mostly of Thoroughbreds, along with some old-fashioned prints of hunting scenes. Finally she set the picture aside. If she ended up somewhere else, the new room would probably have a space where she could hang it. She turned back to her bag and took out several miniature Statue of Liberty figures she had bought for the girls at school.

"Dinner's on the table," Cindy called from the hallway.

"I'll be right there," Allie replied, setting the statues aside. When she returned to the kitchen, the table was set for three, and Ben and Cindy were already seated.

Allie settled into the empty chair, and Ben passed her the dish of chicken. Allie took a generous helping, then waited until the adults had filled their plates before she took a big bite of food.

"I've been doing some horse dealing on my own while you've been gone," Ben told them. Allie was surprised. She knew that when it came to buying race-horses, Cindy was the expert, and Ben never did any business without her being involved.

Cindy raised her eyebrows and tilted her head, waiting for Ben to continue.

"I got a call from a friend in Dubai," Ben went on. "He has a two-year-old colt sired by Champion that he offered me. The dam is an outstanding broodmare whose offspring have set track records in the United Arab Emirates."

"That's fantastic," Cindy said, nodding her approval. "I can hardly wait to get him here."

"It's going to take some time, since he'll have to go through quarantine and the usual tangle of paperwork, but within the next few months we'll have one of Champion's sons at Tall Oaks."

Allie ate in silence, listening to Ben and Cindy discuss the business of running the farm. It felt so nice and normal to be at the table with them, talking about horses and racing.

"Allie's going to help me back Alpine Meadow," Cindy said. Ben looked across the table at Allie.

"So you plan on becoming a horse trainer, too?" he asked.

Allie quickly swallowed her bite of food. "I don't know," she said. "I like helping Chris at Whisperwood, and I like the horses here. It's hard to decide what I want to do."

"You're young," Ben reassured her. "You have plenty of time to figure it out."

Allie saw Cindy's expression go serious for a moment, and she looked down at the table. Maybe Cindy didn't want her to get too attached to either racing or eventing. Maybe she was going to end up someplace where the only horses she rode were from a rental barn.

She finished eating in silence, and when dinner was over, she rose and picked up her dishes, stifling a big yawn.

Cindy gave her a sharp look. "I'd say you need to get to bed," she said.

"I'll do the dishes first," Allie offered. She wanted to

keep the sense she had of Ben, Cindy, and her being a family, and not be sent from the room.

"I'm with Cindy," Ben said. "You looked a little worn out from your busy weekend. I'll help Cindy with the dishes." He stood, then reached over to tousle Allie's hair. "You get a good night's sleep, and tomorrow I'll bring down the pictures my friend sent of Champion's son, Champion's Ghalib."

"Ghalib?" Allie repeated. "That's a funny name."

"It's Arabic for 'victorious,'" Ben said. "I think it's a fitting name for the son of a Triple Crown winner."

Cindy picked up some of the dishes and carried them to the sink. "Some day I'll let you read my diary from the year I was in Dubai," she told Allie. "I learned a few Arabic words while I was there—most of them horse terms that Ben taught me."

Ben picked up the rest of the dishes and followed Cindy to the sink. "That was quite the experience for a young American woman, wasn't it?" he commented. "I think Allie would find your diary very interesting." He turned to Allie and smiled warmly. "Good night, *ata*," he said.

"What's *that* mean?" Allie asked, pausing in the doorway.

111

"It means 'gift,' " Ben said. "You truly are a gift, Allie. I'm very happy that you're here."

"Good night," Allie said, and headed for her bedroom. When she was halfway across the living room, the phone rang.

"Will you get that, Allie?" Cindy called from the kitchen.

"Tall Oaks," Allie said when she picked up the phone.

"I'm calling from New York for Cindy McLean," a woman said. "I realize it's late, but it's very urgent that I speak with her right away regarding our meeting yesterday."

Allie wished she could hang up the phone and pretend it was a wrong number, but instead she only said politely, "I'll get her for you." Going into the kitchen, she told Cindy, "It's an urgent call from New York."

Cindy wheeled away from the sink of dishes and wiped her hands on her jeans before taking the receiver from Allie.

"Hello?" she said, walking from the room as she listened to what the caller had to say.

Allie stayed in the doorway, trying to guess what was going on by what she could hear of the conversation.

"Uh-huh . . . okay," Cindy said, then after a long pause, "We can deal with that." Cindy's voice faded as she walked farther into the living room. In a minute she returned to the kitchen.

"Is there some kind of problem?" Ben asked, turning from the sink, soapy water dripping from his hands. Allie thought it was funny to see Ben at the sink, his shirtsleeves rolled up, but Ben never acted like he was too good to do anything. He absently rubbed a plate with a dish towel while he looked at Cindy.

"It's all going as planned," Cindy said. "It's just coming together more quickly than we expected."

Allie turned to leave the room, feeling as though they were talking over her head. This had something to do with her, but she was being left out.

"Wait a second, Allie," Cindy said, and Allie turned back to see both Ben and Cindy looking at her.

"Are you feeling all right?" Cindy asked her.

Allie took a breath, determined not to tell them what was worrying her, but suddenly the words spilled out in a rush, and there was nothing she could do to stop them.

"I'm afraid you're going to send me away, and

that's what that phone call was about," she said rapidly, then clamped her mouth shut.

Cindy's eyes widened, and she rushed across the room to embrace Allie. "No!" she exclaimed. "I'm not going to send you away, Allie. What would make you think that?"

From over her shoulder, Allie could see Ben nodding in agreement. "We want Tall Oaks to be your home," he confirmed.

"That whole business deal is horse-related," Cindy said. "You don't have anything to worry about, okay?" She stepped back a pace, still holding Allie's arms, and looked into her eyes.

Allie could tell that Cindy was serious, and she nodded slowly.

"Now," Cindy said, releasing her, "you need to get to bed and get a good night's sleep. And remember, you have nothing to worry about."

"Okay," Allie said, and left the room feeling much better. It was clear that Ben and Cindy both wanted her there. But now that she knew Cindy's business dealing involved her *and* horses, she was very curious to know what it was.

8

WHEN ALLIE WOKE UP MONDAY MORNING, RAIN WAS drumming against her bedroom window. She reached over to shut off her alarm, tempted to press the snooze button and drift back to sleep for a few more minutes. Instead she forced herself to get up. She pulled on her clothes and trudged drowsily into the kitchen, where Cindy was pouring herself a cup of coffee.

She turned when Allie walked into the room and wrinkled her nose. "Maybe you should get a little more sleep," she suggested. "You and Melanie won't be riding this morning. The track footing is a bit sloppy."

Allie shook her head stubbornly. "There's lots of other stuff to do," she insisted.

"And you don't have to do it all," Cindy replied. "You aren't at Tall Oaks so you can work yourself into exhaustion, Allison."

"I'm not!" Allie stared at Cindy. "I'd just rather be around the horses than anywhere else."

Cindy gazed at her silently. "Okay," she finally said. "But don't feel like you have to be up before the crack of dawn every single day."

"I'm used to it," Allie said, taking a raincoat off the row of hooks near the kitchen door. "If I slept in, I'd think I was sick."

"I understand that," Cindy said, smiling as she stirred creamer into her travel mug. She glanced out the window. "Melanie is pulling in right now."

"I'll see you at the barn," Allie said, pulling the hood over her hair as she hurried from the house. She dashed through the rain and into the barn, shaking water from her coat when she got inside.

"Nice day if you're a duck," Melanie said, pulling off her own rain jacket. "I'm glad the weather was good for your trip to New York." She looked out the barn door at the pouring rain and sighed. "I just wish it was dry now so I could work Jinx. We only have a couple more weeks before going down to Gulfstream. It's too bad Ben and Cindy don't have a pool here or an indoor arena for exercising." Melanie grimaced. "That is one thing I miss about Townsend Acres."

"What was it like living there?" Allie asked, falling into step beside Melanie as the young jockey started walking up the barn aisle.

"It was kind of weird being around Brad and his trainer." Melanie shuddered. "Ralph Dunkirk is the world's biggest jerk. Still," she said, "the facilities are awesome. Cindy says Ben wants to improve the setup here over the next few years. Tall Oaks is going to be even nicer than Townsend Acres." She grinned. "But then it already is, just because of the people here."

When they reached Jinx's stall, the colt hung his copper-colored nose over the door to sniff at Melanie. "No treats," she told him, then turned to Allie. "I'm going to walk him in the aisle for a few minutes to loosen him up, then give him a massage."

"I'll go get his feed ready," Allie said. "And I'll clean his stall while he's out."

"You don't have to," Melanie said. "I can do it."

"I really don't mind," Allie replied. "Then I'll get Image out and walk her this morning."

"That would be great," Melanie said. "Thanks." She led Jinx from the stall and started down the aisle with him, while Allie quickly cleaned the soiled bedding from his stall. As soon as she had replaced the bedding, she headed for Image's stall. The big black Thoroughbred greeted her with a throaty nicker. "Come on out, girl," Allie said, clipping the lead on Image's halter. "Let's get a little exercise this morning."

For several minutes she led the mare up and down the long, wide aisle, past the empty stalls that lined the barn. When she brought Image through the main stretch of the barn, she saw Melanie and Cindy standing near the office, talking. Cindy waved her over, and Allie brought Image closer. Cindy patted the mare's glossy neck.

"I am really looking forward to breeding her," she said, glancing at Melanie.

Melanie smiled. "I'm so glad you and Ben bought her," she said. "For a while I thought I was going to lose her forever."

Cindy shook her head. "She's back where she belongs," she said. "And she won't ever have to leave."

Allie ran her hand along Image's shoulder, feeling the sleek, warm coat under her hand. "She's so beautiful," she said. "It must have been awful for you when you didn't know what was going to happen with her."

Melanie nodded. "But everything worked out great," she said. "Thanks to Ben and Cindy."

Allie thought about her own situation and nodded. She was sure that between the two of them, Ben and Cindy could take care of anything.

"Melanie and I were just talking about the trip down to Gulfstream for the Fountain of Youth Stakes," Cindy told Allie. "You can spend the week of winter break down there if you really want to go."

"Of course I do!" Allie exclaimed. "I'm part of the McLean Training Stables team, right, Melanie?"

Melanie laughed. "You, Kevin, and me," she said. "And Jinx, of course."

Elizabeth walked by, pushing a wheelbarrow loaded with grain cans. Image twisted her head, trying to keep an eye on the food, and Melanie laughed. "I guess she knows it's breakfast time," she said.

"I'll go put her away and get some other chores done," Allie said.

"I'm heading back to Whitebrook," Melanie told

her. "With some luck we'll be able to get on the track tomorrow morning."

Allie led Image away, feeling more and more like part of the extended family that included the people at Tall Oaks, Whitebrook, and Whisperwood.

When she got to school that morning, Lila and Kendra were waiting by her locker.

"Did you go shopping?" Lila asked as Allie opened her locker. "Did you find any cool clothes?"

Allie shook her head. "We spent most of our time at the track," she admitted.

Kendra looked Allie up and down, then exchanged a long look with Lila. "We need to get this girl into Lexington and do some serious mall time," she said, then turned back to Allie, smiling. "We always have fun trying on clothes and going through the specialty stores," she said. "Could you go if we planned a trip after school one day this week?"

Allie thought about the lesson schedule at Whisperwood and the chores at Tall Oaks, and bit her lower lip. She didn't even know if Cindy would let her go hang out at the mall with the other girls. "I'll have to ask," she said. It did sound like fun, and Cindy had urged her to do things with her friends.

"Let us know," Lila told her as the warning bell for their first class rang. Allie hurried to class, her mind whirling with thoughts about all the horses she wanted to spend time with, and her newfound friends. There had to be a way to do it all, but she didn't know how.

At lunchtime she handed out the statues she had bought.

"That was so sweet of you to think of us," Brittany said, standing her little Statue of Liberty figure on the corner of her lunch tray.

"I'll put her on my knickknack shelf and think of you every time I see her," Roxanne promised.

Allie was glad she had thought of getting each of the girls something, even if it was small. "I'll be sure to check with Cindy about going to the mall," she told Lila after lunch. "It does sound like fun."

That afternoon as she worked with Christina at Whisperwood, helping the students in the beginners' class, she found herself thinking about Alpine Meadow. What would it be like to be the first person on the filly's back? she wondered. If she became a jockey, she could even race the personable filly for Cindy.

As she was helping the students put their horses up, Kaitlin led Sterling Dream into the arena. When

Allie had first started spending time at Whisperwood, Samantha had encouraged her to ride Sterling because Kaitlin had been busy with school activities and wasn't spending a lot of time with the mare. But the times that Allie had ridden Sterling and Kaitlin had come to the barn, the older girl had seemed upset. It wasn't until after Kaitlin had refocused on riding that she had begun to act friendly to Allie.

Now Kaitlin smiled at her. "Do you want to saddle Irish Battleship and do some jumping with me?" she asked.

Allie looked at the empty arena. She hadn't been able to ride that morning, and getting on Irish Battleship sounded wonderful. But there was so much to do at Tall Oaks, and she knew Christina had things to do at Whitebrook. She sighed. "I'd love to," she said. "But Chris is giving me a ride home, so I don't have time."

Kaitlin shrugged. "I know how that is," she said, smiling ruefully. "I had to force myself to make time for riding and not let myself get sidetracked." She patted Sterling's neck. "But I'm glad I did. Giving up on eventing would have been the biggest mistake of my life."

"You really love it, huh?" Allie said.

Kaitlin nodded firmly. "More than anything," she

said. "If I keep working at it, maybe I'll get to be as good as Parker. I'd love to be a part of the United States Equestrian Team."

Allie thought about her own eventing experiences. She knew that, thanks to the lessons her parents had made her take, technically she was a good eventing rider, but she spent more time thinking about the race-horses than about jumping.

"Thanks for asking me to ride with you," Allie told Kaitlin as Christina hobbled across the arena. "Have fun."

When Christina dropped Allie at Tall Oaks, Allie quickly put her books away and hurried down to the barn. Cindy was on the phone when Allie walked past the office, and she paused in the doorway.

"Next week?" Cindy was saying. "That's excellent. I can hardly wait." She glanced up at Allie and nodded toward an empty chair by the door. Allie sat down and waited for Cindy to finish her call.

Cindy was grinning broadly when she hung up the phone. "Sometimes," she said to Allie, "things have the most amazing ways of working out."

"What do you mean?" Allie asked.

Cindy raised her eyebrows. "You'll find out," she said mysteriously.

Allie wasn't worried anymore that Cindy's secret was bad news for her, but she was aching to know what Cindy was up to. *Patience*, she told herself. *You just have to have some patience.*

"We need to talk about your schedule," Cindy said. "I was serious about you helping me with Alpine Meadow, but that means you'll have to start coming home after school instead of working at Whisperwood so much."

Allie pressed her lips together. Christina didn't really need her help with the riding lessons anymore. Kaitlin had been there every day for the last couple of weeks, and she could take care of the things Christina couldn't manage. She nodded slowly. "I'll talk to Samantha and Chris about it," she said.

"If you'd rather keep working with the jumpers, that's fine," Cindy said. "But I think you're trying to do too much."

Allie nodded. "I think I'd rather help you with Alpine Meadow," she said.

Cindy smiled at her. "I can have Rich pick you up after school," she offered. "That way you'll get home a lot sooner than if you take the bus."

"I don't want to bother him," Allie said quickly.

Cindy leaned back in her chair and laughed. "It isn't a bother, Allie. He'll be glad to do it."

Allie remembered Lila's invitation. "Do you think it would be okay if I went to the mall after school one day?" she asked. "Lila and Kendra invited me to go shopping."

Cindy cocked her head, and Allie waited for her to say no.

"I'd like to talk to Lila's parents before you go somewhere with them," Cindy said.

"Her dad is Senator Williams," Allie offered, biting her lower lip nervously. "I met her mom when she picked Lila up after school one day. Mrs. Williams seems really nice."

Cindy nodded. "That makes it easy," she said with a grin. "I've met both her parents at parties Ben's had at the mansion. And you're right—Lila's mom is very nice." She sat back. "I'll call her tomorrow and we'll see what we can figure out so you girls can go have some fun together."

Allie breathed a sigh of relief. "I'm going to visit Alpine Meadow now," she said, and left the office, hurrying through the barn to the chestnut filly's stall.

When she spotted Allie, Alpine Meadow squealed in greeting, making Allie laugh.

"You are such a talker," she told the filly, who stretched her long neck, nuzzling Allie with her soft nose. Allie stepped closer to the stall so that Alpine could rest her chin on Allie's shoulder, and she wrapped her arm around the filly's neck. "I'm going to get on your back soon," she said. "We're going to start training you for the track."

Alpine Meadow exhaled, resting her head heavily on Allie's shoulder. Allie stroked her neck. "You act like it makes you tired just to think about it," she told the filly. "Don't worry, I'm not that heavy."

The rain stopped before Allie and Cindy returned to the house for dinner, and the next morning when Allie got up, the track footing was dry enough to work the horses.

Allie brought Rush Street out to the track as Melanie was struggling with Jinx, who was dancing sideways down the middle of the practice track.

"He's really a stinker this morning," Melanie said, forcing the rambunctious colt to move in a tight circle. Jinx humped his back and kicked out, trying to unseat his rider, but Melanie stuck on him, a determined set to her jaw. After several minutes Jinx settled down, and the girls started warming up the Thoroughbreds.

"You are such a good rider," Allie said, walking Rush Street onto the track. She was glad her mount was calmer and much easier to manage than Jinx, but as she watched Melanie work her colt she thought it would be fun to try riding a more challenging horse.

"All the rotten-mannered horses I've ridden have taught me how to ride well," Melanie said with a chuckle, her attention still focused on Jinx, who looked ready to explode at any moment. "Keep some of that fire for the Fountain of Youth Stakes, boy," she told him. "Putting all that energy into fighting me isn't going to win you any races."

Rush Street moved steadily, ignoring Jinx's antics, and Allie relaxed on his back, enjoying the rocking movement of his long, fluid strides. "I can hardly wait for the race," she told Melanie. "It's going to be really exciting to watch Jinx win a prep race."

"Thanks for the vote of confidence," Melanie said, hauling Jinx's head up as he tried to drop his nose and buck again. "I hope this bit of attitude he's picked up doesn't interfere."

"I'm sure he'll be fine," Allie said. "He just got bored being stuck in the barn yesterday."

"Then let's pick up the pace," Melanie said. Allie

urged Rush Street into a smooth canter, and soon Jinx was even with the other racehorse.

Allie leaned forward over Rush Street's withers, pretending she was in a race, darting an occasional glance at Jinx to check his position. When the chestnut colt started to nose ahead of Allie's mount, she pushed her hands up Rush Street's neck and rose in her stirrups. In response, Rush Street lengthened his strides, and soon the two horses were galloping strongly around the track.

The speed, the feel of the cold wind on her face, and the sound of the horses' hooves pounding on the track gave Allie a boost of adrenaline, and she imagined being on the track with a full field, the grandstands packed with cheering fans.

As they slowed the horses, the high feeling stayed with her, and she left the track in a happy mood that stayed with her all day. She knew she needed to talk to Samantha and Christina and let them know that she had made a decision: she wouldn't be spending as much time at Whisperwood as she had been. All she wanted to do now was work with the racehorses.

When Allie left school that afternoon, Rich was waiting for her in the parking lot, standing by the side of the blue sedan. Allie hurried over to him. "I thought I was supposed to go to Whisperwood this afternoon," she said, confused. "I need to talk to Chris about changing my schedule."

Rich shook his head. "Something's come up at Tall Oaks." He opened the passenger door for her, and Allie climbed into the car, all the worries that had faded away in the last several days coming back in force.

When he got back into the car, Rich quickly put the car in gear and pulled out of the lot.

"What's going on?" Allie asked anxiously. "Is Cindy okay?"

"Everyone is fine," Rich said, looking straight ahead, watching the road carefully as he left town and headed toward the farm. "I was just told to get you home right away."

Allie stared out the windshield. What could have happened to make it so important that she get back to the farm? Then she knew. It was social services—she was certain. She sank back on the seat and stared out the window without seeing any of the passing scenery. This was it. Just when she was feeling good about things, she was going to be taken away.

9

By the time they reached Tall Oaks, Allie was so worried about her uncertain future that she barely noticed that Rich had pulled up by the barn.

"Here you are," he announced, stopping the car.

"Why are we stopping at the barn?" Allie asked, confused.

"Cindy made it quite clear that you were to come straight to the stables," Rich told her, climbing from the car.

Before he could come around to open her door for her, Allie got out, noticing a strange horse van parked near the door. She saw New York license plates on the

130

van. *Champion's colt, Ghalib, must be here*, she realized. Apparently the quarantine process hadn't taken as long as Ben had thought it would. She was eager to see the young horse, but she hesitated, looking at Rich for direction.

"All I was told was to drop you at the barn," Rich told her. "I'll take the car up to the house while you go see what's going on."

Allie walked into the barn and headed for the section reserved for the young horses. But she heard voices from the stallion barn, so she turned and walked rapidly in that direction.

In the distance she saw Ben and Cindy with a strange man, standing in front of one of the stalls. As she got closer she could see a tall chestnut horse moving around in the stall. The horse stopped circling and raised his head, whinnying shrilly.

"I'm sure he'll calm down once he gets used to the change," the stranger told Ben and Cindy. His jacket was embroidered with the name of a horse transportation company. "It was a long trip for him."

Allie hurried over to the small group and stared at the horse. He was definitely older than two, she noted, so he couldn't be Ben's colt from Dubai. The chestnut had a crooked blaze running down his face, which was elegantly shaped. The horse had wide, alert eyes, and his long neck was arched and his ears were pricked as he darted looks around the strange barn. Tension radiated from him as he circled in the box stall, then stopped to whinny again, the sound ringing through the barn.

"Allie," Cindy said, gesturing at the horse, "I'm glad you're here. I'd like you to meet Wonder's Legacy."

The horse tossed his head and pawed at the bedding, then snorted loudly and wheeled around in the stall again.

"He's really upset," Allie commented, eyeing the big Thoroughbred with a frown. The Thoroughbred in front of her might be out of the same dam as Wonder's Star, but he didn't seem to have Star's easy disposition.

The van driver nodded. "The folks at the New York farm said he hasn't left the place in years. Being in the van for so many hours was pretty nerve-racking for him."

"He'll settle in," Cindy said confidently. "Just give him a little time."

Allie felt sympathy for the horse. She remembered the long flight from California to Kentucky, on her way from what had been safe and familiar to a strange new place. At least she had known where she was going. No one could have explained to Legacy where he was going or why.

"It looks like you've got things under control here," the driver said. "Unless there's anything else you need from me, I'll get back on the road."

"Thanks for bringing him on such short notice," Cindy said, smiling at the man. "I'll call the farm in New York and let them know Legacy arrived in good condition."

The shipper left the barn, leaving Allie with Ben and Cindy.

Cindy was frowning. "He didn't have this much *oomph* when Christina and I saw him last year," she said, shaking her head. "I guess the trip upset him."

Allie moved closer to the stall and extended a hand. "Here, boy," she said softly. "You're all right."

Legacy snorted again and tossed his head, but Allie had caught his attention, and he paused to sniff her hand before he struck the floor again with his hoof.

"You need to settle down," Allie said in a quiet, soothing voice, keeping her hand motionless. "You're safe here, you know."

Ben and Cindy stepped back and let Allie talk to the horse, who gradually dropped his head to take in Allie's scent. He drew in a long, loud breath, then released it with a whoosh.

"See?" Allie said, moving closer to the stall. "You're fine."

Legacy lowered his head enough so that Allie could touch his soft muzzle. Slowly she trailed her fingers along his jaw, and the horse took another deep breath and dropped his head a bit more.

"I think you'll have him eating out of your hand in no time," Cindy said, looking relieved.

Ben was nodding slowly, a smile spreading across his handsome face. "I think you made the right call," he said to Cindy.

Before Allie could ask what he meant, voices and footsteps carried through the barn, distracting her. She turned to see Mike, Ashleigh, Christina, and Melanie coming toward them.

"We couldn't wait to see him," Ashleigh said, striding ahead of the others to get to Legacy's stall. She gazed at the horse in silence, then slowly held her hand out. Legacy cautiously sniffed at her hand, then tossed his head again and snorted. "Well," Ashleigh said, "you're not exactly acting like an eight-year-old has-been racehorse, are you?"

Allie turned to her. "Why would you call him that?" she asked.

Ashleigh chuckled, leaving her hand outstretched as she waited for Legacy to calm down. "That's what Brad called him," she told Allie. "But then, he never did have a good eye for what was under the surface."

"That's for sure," Christina said emphatically. "He didn't think much of Star, either."

"Well," Cindy said, "let's hope he keeps feeling that way, because right now we're sharing ownership in Legacy with him."

Mike narrowed his eyes. "Just when we thought we'd cut all ties with Brad as far as Thoroughbred ownership goes . . ." He shook his head, then looked at Ben. "But as I remember, you handled Brad pretty well when you were fighting over ownership of Champion. I'm sure you'll get this worked out, too."

As the adults stood watching Legacy, the colt spun around in his stall again, tossing his head and whinnying.

Allie moved closer to the stall. She felt bad for the Thoroughbred, who seemed confused by his new surroundings.

"It's really all right here," she told the big horse in a quiet voice. "You're going to like it, I promise."

As she kept talking Legacy grew calmer, and after several minutes he was standing quietly near Allie, keeping his attention on her.

"I think you have a new friend," Christina told her. "He really seems to like you."

"I like him, too," Allie said, gently petting the horse's red-gold neck. "I think once he gets used to things he's going to be a sweetheart."

Ashleigh was gazing at Legacy, nodding slowly. "It looks to me like he's picked his groom," she said, glancing at Cindy.

Cindy was smiling, and she nodded. "How about it, Allie?" she asked. "Do you want to take Legacy on as your personal project?"

Allie stared at Cindy. "You mean he'd be like my own horse?" she asked.

"It's going to take some time to get him settled," Cindy said. "He hasn't been handled much in the past couple of years, so he needs a lot of work."

"I think Allie's perfect for the job," Melanie said. "It won't be long before she's riding him."

Allie snapped her head in Melanie's direction. "Ride him?" she repeated.

"That was kind of the plan," Cindy told her. "But we didn't know if you'd want to handle him or not, what with everything else you have going on."

"Was Legacy the reason for the trip to New York?" Allie asked.

Cindy smiled and nodded. "When I found out he was up for sale, I thought he'd be the perfect horse for you. What do you think, Allie? Your own Whitebrook-bred Thoroughbred."

Allie's breath locked in her chest. Cindy had Wonder's Champion, Christina had Wonder's Star, and now she had Wonder's Legacy. She stared at Cindy. "My own horse?" she asked.

Cindy nodded. "I didn't want to push you toward the racehorses when you seem to enjoy eventing so much, but when you said you were more interested in racing, it seemed like perfect timing."

Allie turned to look at Legacy. The stallion was beautiful, with large, intelligent eyes and a long, straight back. Even though he hadn't been worked for a long time, his build was muscular and strong. She knew he was too old to race ever again, but he would be her own to take care of for as long as she was there.

"What do you think, Legacy?" she asked, holding her hand out to him again. As she gazed at him Legacy looked her in the eye, and Allie felt a sudden jolt of understanding, as though Legacy was telling her he had chosen her himself. She reached her hand out slowly, and Legacy pressed his nose into her palm.

"I'll work with him every single day," she told Cindy, her attention still on the horse.

"You'll bring out the best in him," Christina said. She added to Cindy, "I'm so glad you brought him back to Kentucky. I think he and Allie are going to make a great team."

"I agree," Ashleigh said. "I'm looking forward to seeing what you can accomplish with him, Allie. He was a great two-year-old, and with some consistent work, you'll bring out the best in him again."

"We can use him as a training horse on the practice track," Cindy said. "You'll be his official rider—how's that sound?"

Allie couldn't believe she was standing in front of a horse that Ben and Cindy had brought to Tall Oaks especially for her. She stroked Legacy's neck. "We're going to be awesome together, even if we never get to race," she told the horse.

After several minutes the group from Whitebrook left the barn, while Ben and Cindy returned to Cindy's office. Allie stayed behind, unwilling to leave Legacy alone.

"You may not be my very own, but you're my special horse," she murmured to the chestnut, stroking his neck. Legacy sighed and leaned into her hand, clearly enjoying the attention.

That night, after Allie finally left the barn, she went to sleep dreaming of Wonder's Legacy.

For the next several days Allie came home after school every day and went straight to the barn to work with Legacy. She walked him in the barn, getting to know him. With Cindy's help, she worked out a feeding plan for him, and Cindy agreed that Allie should be the only one to feed the horse.

"He'll bond with you that much faster if you're the one who brings him his rations," she told Allie.

When Ashleigh came by one evening to see how Legacy was doing, she stood back and watched Allie handle the stallion. Legacy snuffled Allie's hair, standing calmly as she held his lead, proud to show off to

Ashleigh the progress the horse had made in such a short time. Legacy's coppery coat glistened with the grooming Allie had given him. He was calm and relaxed, although he stayed alert, watching Allie for cues as to what she wanted him to do.

"He looks fantastic," Ashleigh said approvingly as she observed the horse. "I think with your help, his dam's good traits are starting to come out." She sighed. "You're the best thing in the world for him, Allie. I'm so glad Cindy got you and Legacy together."

Allie beamed at the compliment. "I love working with him," she said. "I can hardly wait until I'll be able to ride him."

"It won't be long," Ashleigh said. "He was well trained as a colt, and I'm sure all that will come back in no time. I'm looking forward to seeing you on his back."

After Ashleigh left the barn, Allie turned to Legacy. The big horse eyed her, lowering his head for a caress. "We're going to have a good time together, aren't we, boy?" She sighed happily. Life in Kentucky was turning out to be much better than she had expected.

"We're taking Jinx down to Gulfstream this week," Melanie told her one morning while they were exercising Jinx and Rush Street on the practice track. "Cindy said you'll be able to fly down the first day of your school break."

Allie nodded. "That's going to be fun," she said. She didn't like the idea of leaving Legacy for a week, but she knew the horse would be fine. He seemed very content at the farm now. As the days passed, he seemed to be showing more and more of the traits that Ashleigh said his dam, Wonder, had passed on to most of her foals. Allie wondered what he would have been like as a racehorse if he'd stayed at Whitebrook.

"Maybe," she told him as she groomed him one morning, "when Cindy breeds you to one of the mares here, I'll get to race one of your foals, and we'll have our own Triple Crown winner."

Later that afternoon when Allie went shopping with Lila and Kendra, she had a great time, but she was eager to return to Tall Oaks and see Legacy. Lila and her mother dropped Allie at the farm, and after putting away the clothes she had bought, Allie headed down to the barn. A strange car was parked in front of the building, and she hurried inside to see Cindy and Ben with a tall, dark-haired man in the office.

"I still own a half interest in Legacy," the man said

as Allie walked up to the office. "I just want to check on my investment, Ben."

Allie realized this must be Brad Townsend. After the stories Melanie and Christina had told her about Parker's father, she instantly disliked him.

"You didn't seem to care much about Legacy when he was in New York," Cindy said sharply. "Why the sudden interest now?"

Brad Townsend slowly looked away from Ben to stare at Cindy. "You've made him more accessible to Townsend Acres by bringing him back to Kentucky," he said "We need to discuss the spring breeding schedule. I may want him to cover some of my mares this year."

Allie hurried past the office, going straight to Legacy's stall. "Ben and Cindy won't let Mr. Townsend touch you," she told the horse. Legacy nuzzled her pocket, looking for a treat, and Allie stroked his neck. She knew that Brad had a legal interest in Legacy. Unless he sold out to Ben, he had the right to make decisions about the horse, too. The thought that Brad could take Legacy to Townsend Acres, where she wouldn't be able to see him, upset her, but there was nothing she could do about it. She groaned, burying her face in Legacy's silky mane.

"Just when things are going good, something has to go wrong," she muttered into his neck. "Is anything ever just going to go right for me?"

After several minutes she left Legacy to go back to the office. Brad was gone, and she went inside. Ben and Cindy both looked grim, and Allie sank onto the folding chair near the door.

"Is Mr. Townsend going to take Legacy away?" she asked in a small voice.

Cindy gazed at her from across the desk and slowly shook her head. "As far as I'm concerned," she said, "if he wants to breed any of his mares to Legacy, he can bring them here."

Allie felt relieved. At least Legacy wasn't going to have to leave Tall Oaks. "That's good," she said.

Ben nodded. "It's going to have to be negotiated," he said. "The only reason Brad is concerned about the horse is because we're involved. He hated to lose out on Champion, and he'll do what he can to get even, I'm sure."

"Is there anything you can do?" Allie asked, anxiety over Legacy's well-being sweeping over her.

"I'll get it figured out," Ben said with a reassuring smile.

Cindy nodded in agreement, but the tightness around her eyes didn't change. "Something else has come up, though," she said. "The social worker is on her way over with someone they want you to meet."

Allie stared at Cindy, trying to comprehend what she had said.

"It's Gail Hickam, isn't it?" she demanded. Her biggest fear was becoming reality.

Cindy stared at her. "How did you know about Gail?" she asked.

"I read the letter from social services," Allie burst out. "They're coming to take me away, aren't they?"

Before Cindy could respond, Allie jumped up from the chair. "You told me I didn't have anything to worry about," she said, then fled the office. She ran all the way to Legacy's stall and slipped inside. Legacy snorted softly, startled by Allie's sudden movements.

"I'm sorry I scared you," she said, forcing herself to move slowly. "Cindy kept telling me everything would be fine, and she was wrong. I'll never even get a chance to ride you now." The tears started to flow, and she leaned against Legacy, who curved his neck so that he was cradling her against his shoulder.

After several minutes Allie heard someone outside

the stall, and she pulled away from Legacy to see Ben standing at the door. She looked at him steadily.

"You need to give Cindy a chance to explain," Ben said. "She felt she had good reason for not saying anything to you, Allie. She wasn't trying to hurt you."

Allie stared up at him. "She should have told me," she said defensively.

Ben cocked his head. "You two need to talk about this, but right now Cindy's gone up to the main house to meet our visitors. Do you want to ride up with me?"

Allie shook her head. "I'll walk up," she told him. "I want to spend a little more time with Legacy."

"All right," Ben said. "Don't be too long." With that, he turned and walked away, leaving Allie alone with Legacy.

10

ALLIE SANK DOWN ON THE FLOOR OF THE STALL AND pressed her hands to her face. She wished she could just stay there, but she knew she couldn't hide in the barn forever. She felt a soft nudge on her shoulder and looked up to see Legacy gazing down at her.

"I guess I'd better go back," she told the horse. Legacy nudged her again, and Allie reached up to stroke the crooked blaze that ran down his long nose. "I don't know what's going to happen to me," she said. "But if I have to leave, I'll miss you with all my heart."

She got to her feet and started to leave the stall, stopping as Legacy nickered at her. She turned and

146

wrapped her arms around his neck. "I have to go, boy," she murmured, then squared her shoulders and walked away.

She wondered if she should stop at the cottage and change her clothes before she went up to the mansion, but promptly decided against it. If Gail liked horses, she wouldn't be bothered when Allie showed up smelling like the barn. And if she didn't like them, maybe she'd be put off and just go away. Either way it couldn't hurt.

When she walked onto the broad porch of the house, Allie paused by the pillars that flanked the door, fighting the temptation to turn and run back to the cottage. Then she thought of her parents and stiffened her spine. "I can handle this," she said out loud. "I'll be strong and make you proud of me." She pushed the door open and walked into the slate-floored foyer.

The door into the sitting room was open, and she heard voices from inside. She crossed the entry and paused in the doorway. Ben and Cindy were sitting across from the social worker, a heavyset woman with short gray hair, and beside her Allie saw a tall, elegantly dressed woman with long brown hair.

Cindy glanced up and smiled at Allie. "Come on

147

in," she urged, patting the empty seat beside her. "We've been waiting for you, Allie."

The well-dressed woman rose and smiled warmly at Allie. "Hello, Allison," she said in a throaty voice. "I'm glad I finally get to meet you." She extended her hand to Allie, who stared at the rings on her fingers and the bracelets dangling from her wrist. From Gail's perfect manicure and silk suit, Allie was certain the woman had never cleaned a stall in her life.

"Allie, this is Gail Hickam," Ben said.

"Hi," Allie said uncertainly. She didn't want to like Gail, who looked as though she would fit right in with Brad Townsend and the other rich, snobby people Allie had heard about. But Gail looked very pleasant and friendly, and when Allie glanced down, she saw that Gail had taken her shoes off and was wiggling her toes on the soft carpet. Stuck-up people didn't kick off their shoes in someone else's house.

Gail glanced down and chuckled. "I've been wearing those wretched shoes for hours," she said, pointing at the high heels she had left next to her chair. "I felt so comfortable here that I didn't even think twice about taking them off." She looked back at Allie and smiled. "I'm really pretty casual."

Allie looked at her perfectly manicured nails and held up her hands. "I've been with the horses," she explained. "I don't want to get any dirt on you."

To her surprise, Gail burst out laughing and stepped closer, reaching out to take Allie's hand in hers, giving her fingers a gentle squeeze. "I'm not always this dressed up," she said. "I just returned home from a business trip in Switzerland, where I had to meet with my board of directors. When I got the message from social services, I left the meeting and caught the first flight I could to Kentucky."

Her smile faded. "I was so sorry to hear about your mom and dad, and I'm sorry I wasn't here for you sooner. Because of my work I don't spend a lot of time in the United States, so the first I heard was the letter from social services, which finally caught up with me today."

"So you're really my mom's cousin?" Allie asked, folding her arms in front of her.

Gail sank back onto her chair and tilted her head, looking closely at Allie's face. "I'm actually her second cousin," she said. "Your mom and I only met one time, and that was many years ago. But from what I remember, you look a lot like Jilly."

The social worker leaned forward. "Ms. Hickam runs an import company," she explained to Allie. "She travels all over the world. It's a very exciting life."

"That must keep you very busy," Cindy said to Gail, who nodded.

In the distance, Allie heard the chime of the doorbell, and she started for the door. "I'll see who's here," she said.

But Ben rose and pointed at his chair. "You have a seat and visit," he said. "I'll get it."

Allie sank onto the empty chair next to Cindy and looked across the room at Gail.

"Ms. Hickam has a lovely home in New York," the social worker said.

"I'm just not there very much," Gail added. "I spend several months every year overseas."

Allie looked around the sitting room with its high ceilings and tall windows, and although it was getting dark, she knew the view outside was of the landscaped grounds around the house; beyond that, Tall Oaks' rolling pastures stretched into the distance. She couldn't imagine a life of constant travel. Nothing could be better than waking up here and going out to the barn to spend time with the Thoroughbreds.

Allie looked back to see Gail gazing out the window, nodding as though she knew what Allie was thinking. She glanced at Allie and gave her a little wink. "It must be wonderful living here," she said.

Allie nodded. "It is," she replied.

Voices and footsteps carried into the room from the foyer, and Ben walked back into the sitting room, followed by Mike and Ashleigh. Ben made introductions, and once everyone was seated again, Ashleigh turned to Allie.

"How are things going with Legacy?" she asked.

Allie grinned, happy to talk about the progress she'd been making with the horse. "He's awesome," she said. "He's just like you said Wonder was, sweet and smart."

Gail gave her a curious look. "Is Legacy your horse?" she asked.

Before Allie could respond, the doorbell rang again. Ben stood, laughing. "Maybe I should just stay by the door, since I don't have a butler," he said, shaking his head as he left the room. In a moment he returned with Cindy's parents, Ian and Beth. Tor and Samantha were right behind them. Samantha moved slowly, leaning a little on her tall, blond husband's arm.

"Sammy is going to have twins next month," Allie informed Gail.

"Allie's been helping me with my riding students," Samantha said. "She's a natural with the horses and the kids."

Cindy glanced up at Ben. "Did you decide to throw a party and not tell anyone?" she asked.

"I'm as surprised as you are," he said. "I'll go see if Luis can throw together some refreshments, and if anyone else shows up—" Before he finished the sentence the doorbell rang again. Ben looked at Cindy. "Why don't we move into the main hall?" he suggested. "I'll see who's here now."

Cindy ushered the group out of the sitting room, and as they were walking through the house toward the main dining area, Allie looked over her shoulder to see Christina and Parker, followed by Melanie and Kevin.

Christina was walking without her cane. "This weekend I can start riding again," Christina told her. "We'll get to go on the track together."

"And don't forget we're heading to Gulfstream next week," Kevin told her. "Jinx needs you if he's going to win the Fountain of Youth Stakes."

Gail looked down at Allie. "You have lots of wonderful friends here, don't you?" she asked.

"I do," Allie said. "I love it here."

Gail nodded in understanding. "I can see why," she said. "You're very lucky to have so many people who care about you."

When they reached the dining room, Luis had already set out trays of canapés and drinks. Gail filled a plate with food and sat down next to Allie.

"I don't know much about horses," she told Allie. "Maybe if I come back to visit, you'll teach me how to ride."

Allie set her glass of sparkling cider down and stared at Gail. "You mean you're not going to make me go to New York with you?" she asked.

Gail's mouth dropped open. "And take you away from all this?" She shook her head firmly. "If you were unhappy here and I thought you'd be better off with me, I would do everything I could for you," she said. "But it looks like you have a great life here, Allie." She paused. "Although if you ever want to do some traveling, I'll be glad to take you along on one of my buying trips."

Gail rose and tapped on the side of her glass with a

spoon. The group fell silent, turning their attention to her. "I'd like to say something," she announced.

"First, I'd like to thank you for your hospitality," she said to Ben. Then she addressed the entire group. "I want you all to know that I'm not here to take Allie away. I wouldn't dream of it. She's got a wonderful family right here. The only thing I'd like is to keep up with what's going on and not be left out of her life." She smiled at Allie.

"You're welcome here anytime," Ben said.

"Don't worry," Gail replied, smiling at the crowd. "Wild horses couldn't keep me away from here."

After the impromptu party ended, Allie and Cindy walked back to the cottage together. After Allie had settled into bed for the night, Cindy came into the room.

"Why didn't you tell me that you knew about Gail?" she asked, sitting on the edge of Allie's bed.

Allie sat up and hugged her knees to her chest. "I didn't want you mad at me for reading your mail," she confessed, dropping her chin.

"I was trying to protect you," Cindy admitted. "I didn't want you to get your hopes up about finding family. When Gail didn't respond to social services' inquiries for so long, I was afraid you'd be disappointed and hurt, and I didn't want that to happen." She shook her head. "I'm sorry you've been worried about this for so long. I wish I'd known."

"I don't want to ever leave here," Allie said.

Cindy reached over to touch her cheek. "I love having you here, too." She shook her head. "But if you're worried about something, will you talk to me about it?"

Allie nodded. "Promise," she said.

Cindy smiled. "And if something comes up, I'll tell you about it so we can handle it together. If we talk about things, there won't be any misunderstandings." She rose. "Now you need to get some sleep," she said. "Tomorrow when you get home from school we're going to back Alpine Meadow, and then you're going to ride Legacy."

11

"So Tall Oaks is going to be your permanent home?" Lila asked after Allie told her about meeting Gail Hickam.

Allie raised her shoulders. "The social worker didn't think there'd be any problems," she said. "It sounds like everything is going to work out so I can stay here."

"Awesome!" Lila said, grinning. "Hey, we still haven't gone on our trail ride yet."

"I'll ask Cindy when a good time would be," Allie said. "Tonight I've got a couple of Thoroughbreds to work with."

The girls parted ways, heading for their classes. The day dragged for Allie. She could hardly wait to get home and help Cindy with Alpine Meadow. Then Christina was coming over, and while she rode Rush Street, Allie was going to get on Legacy.

The day finally ended, and Allie hurried out to the parking lot, where Rich was waiting for her. When she got home, she dashed into the cottage to change her clothes, then jogged out to the barn.

Cindy was in her office, going over some paperwork. She glanced up when Allie came into the room. "Are you sure you want to do this?" Cindy asked.

Allie gaped at her. "What do you mean?" she demanded. "I've been thinking about Alpine Meadow all day long."

Cindy nodded. "I just want to be sure that working with the racehorses is what you want to do. I know you enjoyed working with the jumpers over at Sammy's, and I don't want you to feel like you have to help with the Thoroughbreds at Tall Oaks just because you live here."

Allie shook her head and smiled. "It makes me feel a little closer to my dad and mom," she told Cindy. "And it's what I want, too. More than anything."

"Okay, then," Cindy said, rising. "You get Alpine Meadow's halter and lead, and I'll meet you at her stall."

Allie hurried to the tack room, then strode through the barn to where Cindy was in the chestnut filly's stall, waiting. Allie let Alpine sniff her over, and she gave the filly's poll a gentle rub. "You're going to be a doll about this, aren't you?" she said.

Although Allie had never backed a racehorse, she had seen both of her parents help trainers with the first step of getting a Thoroughbred used to the weight of a rider. She waited until Cindy had Alpine Meadow haltered, and Allie moved to the filly's side, draping her arms over her back. Alpine turned her head to eye Allie curiously.

"She's nice and calm," Cindy said, stroking the filly's sleek shoulder. "I don't think we're going to have a problem in the world with this one." She nodded to Allie and held out her hand so that Allie could push herself higher, resting her weight on the filly.

Alpine shifted her weight and tossed her head, pawing at the stall floor, but she didn't move, and for several minutes Allie lay over her back, stroking her shoulder.

"You're the best filly in the world," she said softly.

"That's enough for now," Cindy finally said, and Allie slipped to the ground. Cindy was grinning, petting the filly as she looked at Allie. "She's going to be a cinch to saddle-train," she said. "And with any luck, she'll be a knockout on the track."

"I hope so," Allie said. "I plan to be her jockey." She dug a chunk of carrot from her jeans pocket and fed it to Alpine, who crunched the treat contentedly. "We're going to raise all kinds of money for the Children's Rescue Fund, aren't we, girl?"

Alpine Meadow bobbed her head and nuzzled Allie's hands, searching for more treats. "That's it," Allie said. "I don't want to spoil your dinner. Besides," she added, "now that you're going into training, we'll need to work out a special feeding plan for you, won't we?" She turned to Cindy.

Cindy nodded. "We'll work on it together," she said. "Now, if you want to get your tack, we'll take Legacy out to the track."

While Allie was in the tack room, she heard a car pull up to the barn, and she came out to see Christina striding through the door. She still had a little limp, and Allie eyed her leg with a frown.

"It's fine," Christina said in response to Allie's look. "All I need to do now is build up the muscles in my leg. Some easy riding will do me good."

"Do you want me to tack Rush Street for you?" Allie asked, then grinned. "Or would you prefer to ride Dove?" Ben had bought the Arabian mare for Cindy. A veteran lesson horse for handicapped riders, Dove was the calmest, gentlest horse Allie had ever been on.

"No!" Christina exclaimed. "I'll leave the bombproof babysitting horse for someone else. I'll tack up a race-horse, if you don't mind."

Allie laughed. "I'll get Rush Street in the cross ties for you," she said, then hurried through the barn to Legacy's stall.

"We're going riding, boy," she told the horse, who eyed the tack curiously. Before she got Legacy out, Allie readied Rush Street for Christina. By the time Christina came through the barn with her tack, Allie had Legacy tied in front of his stall and was brushing him thoroughly.

"He looks fantastic," Christina said. "I don't think he's the same horse Cindy and I saw in New York last year. He looks so content."

"He's a great horse," Allie replied.

"He's definitely thriving under your care," Christina said. "He might not have been the right horse for me, but I think the two of you make a great pair." She left Allie to finish tacking Legacy and carried her tack over to Rush Street.

Allie settled the saddle pad onto Legacy's back, waiting for the horse to react. But Legacy stood quietly, letting her fuss over the position of the pad. When he felt the weight of the saddle, he raised his head, angling it so that he could see what Allie was doing.

"It's just your saddle, big guy," she said calmly, reaching under him to tighten the girth. Legacy inhaled deeply, and Allie let the girth go loose. "I'm not going to pinch you with it," she told the horse, waiting for him to relax before she fastened the girth. After a few minutes Legacy let her finish tacking him, taking the bit willingly, and as she led him from the barn he danced a bit.

"Look at that," Cindy said from where she was waiting by the track. "He looks like a three-year-old ready for his first race."

Legacy tossed his head, testing the air, and Allie grinned. "You're not an old has-been, are you?"

Christina came out with Rush Street, and Cindy

161

boosted her onto the saddle, then turned to Allie. "Let me keep a grip on him until we know he's going to behave," she said. "I know you're a good rider, and he isn't exactly green, but I don't know what's been done with him before he got here."

Allie nodded. She wasn't worried at all about Legacy acting up, but she knew Cindy was being cautious for Allie's safety. She buckled her helmet into place and let Cindy give her a leg up. She sat quietly in the saddle, waiting to see how Legacy was going to react. The big chestnut swiveled his head around to sniff Allie's boot, then pulled against Cindy's hold on his reins, trying to get onto the track.

"I think he's fine," Allie said. "I'm sure I can handle him."

Cindy reluctantly let go of the reins, and Allie guided the Thoroughbred onto the track. When he saw Rush Street, Legacy pranced a bit, tugging at the reins. "Settle down," Allie told the horse. "We're going for an easy jog, not a race."

As they circled the track, Legacy settled into a steady pace. "It's like he remembers everything he's supposed to do," Allie said, delighted with how well behaved the stallion was.

Christina nodded, keeping Rush Street from nosing ahead of Legacy as they rode the oval. "He's a great horse," she said.

"And someday," Allie said, "I'll be racing on his foals."

"So you're definitely going to work at becoming a jockey?" Christina asked.

Allie nodded firmly. "Absolutely," she said, patting Legacy's neck. "And if I work hard enough, maybe I'll be as good a jockey as my mom and dad were."

Christina glanced over at Allie and Legacy and smiled. "You've got a good start on it," she said.

After they had walked the horses for several minutes, Cindy called them off the track. "That was a great first ride for both of you," she said. To Allie she added, "When you get back from Gulfstream, we'll start taking Legacy on the trails and condition him. He may not be racing anymore, but we want our new stallion in top shape."

As Allie hopped from Legacy's back, Ben pulled up to the barn in his sports car. He climbed out and strode over to the track, a broad grin splitting his face. He held a manila envelope in his hand.

"What's that?" Cindy asked, looking at him curiously.

"Legacy's papers," Ben announced, waving the envelope. "I just paid a visit to Brad and worked out a deal." He grimaced at Cindy. "I did have to give up a breeding with Champion to a Townsend Acres mare, live foal guarantee," he said. "But it seemed a small enough price to pay for knowing that Brad won't have any hold on Legacy."

"So Legacy belongs to Tall Oaks?" Allie asked, resting her hand on the horse's shoulder.

Ben shook his head. "No," he said. "Legacy belongs to you, Allie."

"Me?" Allie felt a rush of confusion and hope. She thought of Legacy as hers anyway, but she couldn't imagine anyone actually giving her ownership of this amazing and valuable horse!

"That's right," Ben said. "I had the papers corrected to show you, Allison Avery, as Legacy's legal owner."

Allie stared at Ben. "Why would you do that?" she asked.

"Because Legacy needs you as much as you need a horse of your own," Ben said.

Cindy nodded in agreement. "And this is home for both of you now," she said, smiling contentedly. "No one is going to take either of you away, and that's that."

Allie stroked Legacy's sleek neck. "Did you hear that?" she asked him. "You're mine, Legacy." She turned to Ben and Cindy with a grin. "Thank you both so much," she said, feeling the urge to cry with happiness. She swallowed hard and raised her chin. "I can't tell you what this means to me."

Ben and Cindy nodded. "It's our pleasure, Allie. It really is. Now, you'd better go tend to your horse."

Allie nodded with excitement. "I need to go put my horse up!" she said. "Then I have some chores to do before I do my homework." She started to walk away, then turned back to Cindy. "Would it be okay if I invited Lila to come home with me after school one day this week?"

Cindy nodded, her smile bright. "Of course," she said.

Allie led Legacy off, walking calmly, but when they were out of sight in the barn, she stopped, flinging her arms around the horse's neck. "Did you hear that, Legacy?" she asked. "We're both home, and we're going to stay here, forever."

Unbeaten filly Meadow Star, with jockey Chris Antley, wins the $112,600 Comely Stakes at Aqueduct Raceway in New York on March 30, 1991.

MEADOW STAR
1988–2002

Described by her handlers as very kind and sweet, the chestnut filly Meadow Star had seven wins in seven starts during her two-year-old season and four more as a three-year-old. While most of her wins were by several lengths, her Mother Goose Stakes race against Lite Light was so close it took the judges six minutes to name Meadow Star the victor. She was named the champion two-year-old filly of 1990, then Florida's champion three-year-old filly, but those honors were not the chestnut filly's greatest claim to fame. A few weeks before the 1990 Breeders' Cup, Meadow Star's owner, Carl Icahn, announced his plan to donate all of her winnings to the Children's Rescue Fund, an organization he founded to help homeless children. During her racing career, Meadow Star's purses made over $900,000 for the fund.

Meadow Star retired to Trackside Farm at the end of her four-year-old season and died of foaling complications in 2002. While her name isn't well known to many racing fans, the money she raised to help needy children makes her legacy a very special one.

Mary Newhall spent her childhood exploring back roads and trails on horseback with her best friend. She now lives with her family and horses on Washington State's Olympic Peninsula. Mary has written novels and short stories for both adults and young adults.